**'Goodnight, V**

Mark swayed over
away. Verity caug
tension inside her throbbing.

'Thank you, Mark, for a wonderful evening,' she almost gasped. Was she being a gullible fool? Leaving herself open to more disillusionment, more hurt?

'It's only whetted my appetite for more evenings,' Mark said gallantly, his face blurring above hers. He whispered, 'I've enjoyed it,' and, before she could even blink, he was gone.

**Dear Reader**

This is the time of year when thoughts turn to sun, sand and the sea. This summer, Mills & Boon will bring you at least two of those elements in a duet of stories by popular authors Emma Darcy and Sandra Marton. Look out next month for our collection of two exciting, exotic and sensual desert romances, which bring Arab princes, lashings of sun and sand (and maybe even the odd oasis) right to your door!

*The Editor*

**Elizabeth Duke** was brought up in the foothills of Adelaide, South Australia, but has lived in Melbourne ever since her marriage to husband John. She trained as a librarian and has worked in various libraries over the years. These days she only works one day a week, as a medical librarian, which gives her time to do what she loves doing most—writing. She also enjoys researching her books and travelling with her husband in Australia and overseas. Their two grown-up children are now married.

**Recent titles by the same author:**

BOGUS BRIDE

# SHATTERED WEDDING

BY
ELIZABETH DUKE

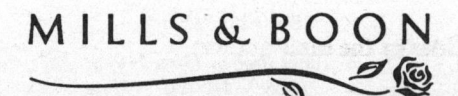

MILLS & BOON

MILLS & BOON LIMITED
ETON HOUSE, 18-24 PARADISE ROAD
RICHMOND, SURREY TW9 1SR

**DID YOU PURCHASE THIS BOOK WITHOUT A COVER?**

If you did, you should be aware it is **stolen property** as it was reported *unsold and destroyed* by a retailer. Neither the Author nor the publisher has received any payment for this book.

*All the characters in this book have no existence outside the imagination of the Author, and have no relation whatsoever to anyone bearing the same name or names. They are not even distantly inspired by any individual known or unknown to the Author, and all the incidents are pure invention.*

*All Rights Reserved. The text of this publication or any part thereof may not be reproduced or transmitted in any form or by any means, electronic or mechanical, including photocopying, recording, storage in an information retrieval system, or otherwise, without the written permission of the publisher.*

*This book is sold subject to the condition that it shall not, by way of trade or otherwise, be lent, resold, hired out or otherwise circulated without the prior consent of the publisher in any form of binding or cover other than that in which it is published and without a similar condition including this condition being imposed on the subsequent purchaser.*

*MILLS & BOON and the Rose Device are trademarks of the publisher.*

*First published in Great Britain 1994 by Mills & Boon Limited*

© Elizabeth Duke 1994

*Australian copyright 1994   Philippine copyright 1994
This edition 1994*

ISBN 0 263 78550 5

*Set in Times Roman 10 on 11¼ pt.
01-9407-57646 C*

*Made and printed in Great Britain*

# CHAPTER ONE

VERITY didn't see the man step on to the escalator behind her as she rode up to the hotel's mezzanine floor. Her gaze was fixed to the huge tapestry covering the wall of the gallery above.

She never ceased to be proud that she was the one responsible for that stunning feature wall—perhaps the most talked-about feature of her father's splendid hotel. She, as the hotel's interior designer, had commissioned the tapestry, suggested the colour-scheme, even had a say in its design. People were impressed, proud that this breathtaking work of art was Australian-made, Australian-designed. The experts, hailing the tapestry as a masterpiece, said it was as good as anything they had seen in Paris or Rome or Madrid.

But the tapestry wasn't what she had come up here to see. She walked swiftly past, across the carpeted gallery to the hotel's elegant ballroom. There was a medical conference at the hotel this week, and tonight the delegates were holding their gala dinner.

The room, already set up for the dinner, was a sea of pristine white tablecloths gleaming with silver and crystal under the graceful overhead chandeliers.

This was the first time the ballroom had been used since an electrical fault had caused a near-disastrous fire a few months ago. The efficient sprinkler system had quickly put out the fire, but the water had caused almost as much damage to the carpet and the floor-to-ceiling curtains as the fire itself. Verity had overseen the refurbishments—new colour scheme, new curtains, new carpet, repainting. It had been quite a job. Now it looked even better than it had before.

She had checked the ballroom already, numerous times. But now she just wanted to see how it looked, set up in all its glory for its first big function since the fire.

Magnificent, she thought, well satisfied. Melbourne's leading florist had come in personally to do the floral arrangements, and they were as dramatic and innovative as always, with delicate silk butterflies dancing among the fresh blooms.

Marvelling at the florist's genius, Verity moved forward to inspect the nearest arrangement more closely. She couldn't resist reaching up to touch one of the butterflies. They looked so real!

She jumped as a male voice drawled from behind;

'You've done a great job. You should feel mighty proud of yourself.'

She swung her head round, her startled blue eyes meeting other eyes as grey as polished pewter. His accent was... hard to identify. American? English? There were aspects of both in the attractively deep voice.

'Thank you,' she said faintly, wondering how he knew she was the one responsible for the ballroom's interior design. *She* certainly hadn't spread it around. And she knew her father wouldn't have either. For a wealthy tycoon—one of the richest men in Australia—her father was very low-key, very protective of his family's privacy, avoiding personal publicity like the plague. Even in business circles he was known as the 'quiet achiever'— and was highly respected for it.

So who *was* this man? Verity blinked up at him, struck by the fact that, though she was tall, he was taller, and faintly stunned by... what was it exactly? What was it about him that made her breath threaten to seize up her throat? It was very strange. Disconcerting. She wasn't used to men affecting her like this, leaving her so breathless, so aware, so... unsure. A perfect stranger!

She found herself dissecting him bit by bit, trying to work it out. His face wasn't so remarkable, except for those compelling grey eyes. His features were craggy, his mouth rather crooked, his eyebrows heavy under his wavy mid-brown hair, one eyebrow having a decidedly arrogant tilt. His jaw was firm, a strong jaw, but no, it wasn't his face...

His height, then? The hint of power in the lithe, well-proportioned body? But she'd seen tall, lithe, well-built men before and they'd never struck her as forcibly as this.

The way he moved? Now that... Verity bit her lip as he took a step closer, his hand half raised at his side. The smooth motion of his body, the angle of his arm, the tigerish grace of the man... she found herself mesmerised. The man exuded some powerful force from within him that was arrestingly potent, heart-stoppingly male.

She swallowed, sensing that here could be a dangerous man. Was he aware of it, of the seductive power he projected? She flicked her tongue over suddenly dry lips. Pitting her wits against such a man would be a new, heady experience for Verity Danza. Until now she had always been in control of every situation she'd found herself in, always able to hold her own with any man, never entirely losing her head or her heart, even during the time she had been engaged to Donald, even during their most intimate moments. It would be exciting to see if this man had the power to...

She shivered, feeling a sudden, illogical flare of panic. Let's hope he's just visiting, she thought wildly... a casual tourist from overseas. Or safely married, with a string of kids. She had never looked at a married man, and she didn't intend to start now, no matter how tempted.

'Have you been in the floral business for long?' He indicated the floral display with an admiring sweep of his hand. 'You're very good at it. I've never seen such a superb arrangement. You must be greatly in demand.'

Realisation hit her, and it took an effort not to gape at him. He thought she was the hotel's florist! He had no idea who she really was.

Rather than feeling affronted, her heart soared, and she gave him a dazzling smile. He was being friendly out of genuine courtesy, genuine admiration—not because he knew she was Lorenzo Danza's daughter! So many men, she mused with a hidden sigh, had no interest in her as a *person*—they only sought her company because of her father's immense wealth and power.

Donald Makim being a classic case in point, she mused, her smile losing some of its sparkle. He had managed to hide his true colours better and for longer than most, almost sweeping her to the altar before he'd been exposed, mercifully, for what he was.

From under her fringe of dark lashes she studied the grey-eyed stranger, the man who thought she was here to do the flowers. He was bound to be no different from the others, she thought cynically, once he found out who she was. He would either scuttle for cover, as the nicer ones usually did, or he would be all over her like a rash. Somehow, knowing a girl was an heiress always *did* make a difference to a man. Damn them!

'You're very kind,' she said, flashing another smile, deciding not to spoil things by enlightening him. Anyway, why bother? She would probably never see him again. A pity, she found herself thinking.

'Are you on the hotel staff?' she asked. She didn't think so for a minute—she knew most of the staff by now, by sight at least. Besides, the man's accent suggested that he was more likely to be a guest of the hotel, a visiting tourist, as she'd suspected. But if he was, why was he here in the ballroom at this hour of the day?

Her natural caution, heightened by her recent disillusionment, her mistrust of men, whispered a warning. Had he seen her heading this way? Surely he couldn't have *followed* her here?

'Perhaps I should introduce myself,' he said, seeming to realise that his presence in the ballroom was puzzling her. 'Dr Mark Bannister, from California. I'm here for the paediatrics congress.'

'Ah.' Verity's brow cleared, and she raised a slender hand to run her fingers through her long silky black hair—a habit she had unknowingly fallen into, a sign that her tension was easing. 'Oh...well, I won't hold you up,' she said hastily. But she paused a moment longer, finding herself reluctant to leave him. 'Er—are you looking for someone?'

'Oh, no, nothing like that.' His lips eased into a smile, doing wonderful things to his eyes, and causing the deep cynical lines down his cheeks and the smaller lines round his eyes to break up into soft wrinkles, radiating over the gently tanned skin. She was conscious of a tiny quiver in response. Dr Mark Bannister, she thought, is a *very* attractive man.

'I just popped in to have a look at the set-up in here,' he said, glancing round. 'I'm giving an address at the dinner tonight.'

'Oh.' Her earlier thought that he might have followed her here evaporated. 'Well, I'll leave you to it, then.' She glanced at her watch. 'I'm due at the Children's Hospital in half an hour.' Now why on earth had she told him *that*? Because he was a doctor, a *children's* doctor? Because she wanted to prolong her time with him? Because wildly, irrationally, she would say anything in the hope of seeing him again!

'You do the flowers at the hospital too?' he asked, looking impressed.

She laughed. 'No. I'm just...visiting.'

He touched her arm, the light contact sending an odd little ripple of pleasure through her. 'Look, I need to go the Children's Hospital myself. Why don't we go together?'

Verity's heart jumped. 'You do?' Her native scepticism brought a faint niggle of doubt, but she dismissed it. He was a visitor to Melbourne, a conference delegate who had come all the way from America. He couldn't possibly know who she was. He'd probably never even heard the name Danza. 'You have an appointment there?' she asked him. 'Or do you just want to have a look at the hospital while you're here?'

'Both,' he said easily. 'I do want to have a look at the hospital, but I also happen to have an appointment with the medical director there, at three o'clock. They're interested in some work I've been doing.'

'Oh.' She let that sink in. If the Children's Hospital was interested in his work... 'Then you *are* a children's doctor?' she said involuntarily. 'I mean—a paediatrician?' she corrected herself.

He nodded, his lip quirking at the correction. She hid her own amusement. He was probably surprised that she even knew what the word meant. A mere florist!

She was tempted to ask more questions, but time was slipping by. 'Um...are you ready to go?' she asked, almost shyly. 'Have you seen enough here?'

'Enough...for now.' He was looking at *her* as he said it, and she found herself actually blushing—something she hadn't done for many years. 'Shall we take a taxi?' he asked. 'Or do you have your car here? Or...van?' he amended, obviously still under the impression that she was a florist.

'I have my car. I didn't actually do these flowers myself,' she heard herself admitting. 'I just popped in to...to check that everything had been done right.' That at least was the truth...as far as it went.

'Ah, I might have guessed you were the artist-in-chief, the mastermind behind these magnificent arrangements. The...designer, would you call yourself?' He cocked an eyebrow at her.

She seized on the word. 'Yes, you could call me that,' she said, and smiled to herself. Well, it was true, she *was* a designer. She disliked lying to people, and for some reason she didn't want to lie to *this* man. Giving a mistaken impression to protect herself was one thing, but blatantly lying, when there was no real reason for it, was entirely different.

'Look...' She made a sudden decision. 'I'll bring my car round to the front entrance and pick you up there in—say, ten minutes?' If he walked down to the basement car park with her, he would see her reserved car space. A florist—even the manager of the business—wasn't likely to have a spot reserved for her in the executive section of the hotel car park! And she didn't want her real identity revealed just yet.

'Er—may I know your name?' he asked, the corner of his mouth curving upward. 'If I'm to accept a lift from a stranger, I feel I should know at least that much about you.'

She laughed—a joyful tinkling sound. He had a sense of humour as well! Her heart soared anew.

'Everyone just calls me...Verity,' she said airily. No need at this stage to be more specific.

The American showed no sign that he had heard the name before, or that he connected it with the name Danza.

'Verity...pretty name. Most suitable for a famous florist.'

She flushed. This wasn't right. She just couldn't let him go on believing that she was something she wasn't. Not now that they were going to meet up again, if only for a short car ride.

'I'm afraid I...I've allowed you to assume...' She faltered, and started again. 'I'm not a florist, actually,' she rushed on. 'I had nothing to do with these floral arrangements, except perhaps for the basic colour scheme. I'm an interior designer. There was a fire in the ballroom recently, you see, and I—well, I've been doing the refurbishing.' No need to say any more, to tell him that she was the one who had chosen the décor for the entire hotel.

'Oops! I've made a bit of a fool of myself, haven't I?'

His response charmed her anew. 'It was my fault——'

'Not at all. Why should you open up to a complete stranger? A girl can't be too careful, especially when strange men come sneaking up from behind without warning!'

They were both laughing—Verity with relief—as they left the ballroom together. She was still smiling as she waved him to the escalator.

'See you downstairs. Give me ten minutes.' She swung away from him and headed for the lifts. As she rode down to the basement car park, she tried to stifle a rare stir of excitement.

Steady on! He's bound to be married—the nicest men always are. He'll be happily married, with kids, there's nothing surer. He must like children, or he wouldn't be a paediatrician. She sighed as she stepped from the lift. She hadn't met an attractive doctor yet who wasn't married by the age of thirty. And Dr Mark Bannister would have to be over thirty—close to his mid-thirties, at a guess.

It was a sobering thought. Why was it that the nicest, most genuine guys were always married, she wondered... snapped up by lucky girls who didn't have the terrible burden of the Danza name? In her case men either ran for their lives or else they got dollar signs in their eyes.

Her lips tightened as she hurried to her car. She'd been burnt once already by a fortune-hunter. A cheating womaniser to boot. Donald Makim, the man she had almost married, had completely fooled her. And yet she had been so sure, poor fool she, that he was different from the others. Donald was the only man she had ever considered marrying, the only man she had ever slept with—and that was only after they had become engaged.

She could thank her famous cool, her self-control—and her stubborn Danza pride—for seeing her through that dark period of her life. She had managed to survive her broken engagement to Donald, to survive the shock of discovering that he was two-timing her, involved with other women, even while he was pledging undying love to her. No amount of pleading, of denying it, of later breaking down and throwing himself at her feet in sheer desperation, swearing that the other women had meant nothing to him, that she was the only woman he wanted or would ever want, had touched her. Donald had wanted her for her money, her name, her connections, for the power all those things would bring him... nothing else.

For a second she sagged against the door of her car—a modest white Mazda sedan, a car that few people would look at twice. She was older and wiser now, more on her guard than ever. She would never let another man fool her the way Donald had. Never! Perhaps she would never again be able fully to trust another man.

Best to keep her experience with Donald in mind when she met up again with Dr Mark Bannister ten minutes from now. No matter how attractive she found him, and no matter how many times they might meet in the limited time he was here in Melbourne, she had no intention of losing her head. Still less her heart!

'Ever been to Australia before?' she asked him as she eased the Mazda into the stream of traffic.

'I have to confess, this is the first trip I've made down here. I've always wanted to come.'

'You have?'

'Sure... I've wanted to come for a long time, but I guess I was just too busy.'

'Are you here for very long?' She tried to keep the question casual, but a faint huskiness crept into her voice as she spoke. She hoped he hadn't noticed it.

'I'm not sure how long I'll be here. Maybe a year, maybe longer.'

A year! She couldn't believe it.

'I thought you were only here for the medical conference,' she said, aware of her quickening heartbeat. 'You're planning to travel around Australia while you're here? See something of the country?'

'Well, I'd like that, sure. But actually, I'm here to work. Nothing's finalised yet, but I hope to give some lectures, run a few seminars, share my expertise with a number of organisations. I was already coming to Melbourne anyway, to present a paper at this paediatrics congress. The medical staff at the Children's Hospital heard about my visit and they're keen to pick my brains while I'm here. That's why I'm going there now, to work out a programme.'

'You must be an expert in your field. An expert in... children's diseases?' Verity glanced enquiringly at him.

'My special interest is childhood asthma. Sadly, there are still far too many children—and adults too, for that matter—dying from the disease.'

Aware of a new intensity in his voice, Verity flicked him a glance sideways, and in the instant before her gaze swung back to the road she saw that he was frowning, a brooding look darkening his eyes. Obviously this man cared deeply about his chosen work. Whatever had motivated him to specialise in his particular field, he wasn't in it simply for the money, the glory...he genuinely cared, she was sure of it.

She found her admiration for him growing.

'So you won't have much spare time, then,' she ventured, 'to see the sights we have to offer in and around Melbourne, let alone the rest of Australia?'

She kept her face averted, but even without looking round, she knew he'd turned to face her. When he spoke, the bleak note in his voice had vanished.

'I wouldn't say that. All work and no play, they say...' He paused, and she realised she was holding her breath. 'When the conference finishes on Friday, I intend to take a few days off to look around, have a bit of a holiday. I'm sure the hospital won't expect me to start work immediately. These programmes take time to organise...they need to be scheduled well in advance.'

Verity swallowed. 'I suppose you'll want to go up to Sydney, or to the Gold Coast...' Tourists were always keen to see Sydney's beautiful harbour and stunning Opera House, while the fabulous beaches of Queensland and the glories of the Great Barrier Reef were normally an irresistible enticement to overseas visitors.

'I've already been to Sydney. I was there for a week before the conference started.' She sensed a change in his tone, a hint of...derision? Mockery? Had he heard the yearning note in her voice? she wondered in faint alarm.

'And I've no great wish to spend my time lazing on a beach,' he drawled. 'I want to see something of

Melbourne, if I'm to work here... get to know the place a bit better. And maybe do some day trips out of town.'

Her heart gave a flutter. She bit back the offer that rose to her lips. Don't push it, she cautioned herself, even as she wondered idly *why* she was so keen to see him again, this stranger, this American who was only in Australia for a limited time. Maybe that was the very reason! She could enjoy his company without too much thought to the future... or his motives... or whether he was a man she could trust.

'Where are you staying?' she asked lightly. 'At the hotel?'

'Yes, at the Star. It's a fine hotel. I'm most impressed. The staff sure make you feel welcome. They even address you by name... I don't know how they do it.'

Verity felt a surge of pride. Her father's hotel had always had a fine reputation, and the friendliness and courtesy of the staff there was fast becoming legendary. But to hear Mark Bannister praising it, when he had no idea who she was... It meant a lot to her.

'And you...' She felt his eyes on her as he spoke, but his tone was careless, his face impassive. 'You live close to the city? Or out in the suburbs?'

She hesitated, thinking of her father. He'd have a fit if she answered such a question from a stranger, especially a man she had virtually bumped into by accident. But somehow, Mark didn't seem like a stranger, not any more. Still, there was no need to be too specific.

'I have a flat here in town,' she told him. No need to tell him where exactly. If he knew she had an apartment in the Star Tower, the Star Hotel's twin tower, right here in the central business district of Melbourne, he'd wonder how on earth she could afford such a location. It would mean having to tell him who she was, and she didn't want to do that, take that risk just yet. It might frighten him away. Or change his thinking, his attitude towards her.

As if sensing her reluctance, he didn't ask where it was. No doubt he thought she was just being cautious, not volunteering her address to a stranger.

'I'm usually only in town during the week,' she hastened on. 'I go home to our house in the country at weekends, or whenever I can.'

'Ah, a country girl.'

She glanced at him, caught a faint glimmer in his eyes, and wondered what he was thinking. Did he see her now as a simple country girl? She felt amusement tug at her lips. First a florist, now a farm girl! Would he be disappointed when—*if*, caution made her correct herself— he learnt the truth?

Surely he wouldn't. He was a sophisticated man of the world...a renowned paediatrician, surely accustomed to moving in any circles. A man like Dr Mark Bannister wasn't likely to be awed by her family name, her family's wealth, and the power that went with it...or, on the other hand, be repelled by it, as some people were, thinking the Danzas must be insufferable snobs and Verity Danza a spoilt, pampered brat. Why should it affect this man, this commanding, self-assured medical expert from America, in any way? He must be a wealthy man in his own right.

All the same...it might be wise to keep the truth to herself for as long as she could.

## CHAPTER TWO

'Do you want me to wait for you?' Verity asked as she parked the car in the hospital car park and walked with Mark to the main entrance.

He looked down at her, and she felt her pulses leap as her eyes met his. She tried to read what was in the grey depths, but his expression was inscrutable. She felt tension knotting her stomach. Wary as she was of getting involved with any man again, she didn't want this man to go out of her life, she realised. This was a vital moment—it could be their last moment together if he didn't feel the same stir of interest that she did. She tried to project that thought with the force of her gaze.

'I'm not sure how long I'll be,' he said at length, his gaze flicking away from hers, abruptly severing the direct contact between them. 'You'd better not wait. I'll get a cab back to the hotel.'

She panicked. Wasn't he even going to ask how he could get in touch with her again? Swallowing, she heard herself offering, 'Maybe I could show you some of our sights, when your conference is over?'

His gaze slid back to her, the grey eyes shadowed by his half-closed lids. Not answering at once, he waved her through the glass doors into the hospital's foyer. Once inside, he drew her to one side—by which time she was in a fever of suspense, her anxiety so acute that she was able to blot from her mind the fact that she was brazenly chasing after a man for the first time in her life.

'Well, now, that's mighty kind of you, Verity. But I can't let you do anything else for me.'

She felt dismay wash over her. This is goodbye...he doesn't want to see me again. He's going to be too busy...or he doesn't care enough. Men like Dr Mark Bannister must have females chasing after them all the time.

'Now it's my turn. I'd like to show my thanks to *you* in some way,' he added smoothly, and it was a moment before she realised what he was saying, what he meant. 'I've been given a couple of tickets to a jazz concert at the Concert Hall tomorrow night. James Morrison's the star attraction. I was going to ask one of the other guys from the conference, but I'd much rather ask you, Verity...if you'd like to come.'

She blinked up at him, dazed for a magical second.

Years of studied self-composure, of never letting anything puncture her cool assurance, came to her rescue. She said coolly, 'That sounds lovely. You like jazz?'

'Sure do. Do you?'

'Yes!' Fancy him liking jazz too! So many people didn't—it left them cold. 'I just adore James Morrison,' she enthused. 'He's a genius. He can do anything with any instrument he plays!'

'I agree. I heard him play in the States when he was over there.'

'You did?'

Before she could get any more carried away, and start firing more questions at him, he said quietly, 'I'd better let you go and visit your friend...or friend's child, or whoever.'

She nodded, sheer habit preventing her from volunteering the truth—that she had been a voluntary helper at the hospital for some time now, coming here twice a week to sit with young children who had no parents or family of their own to visit them. She had always taken great care not to publicise it. People—the media in particular—tended to make such a song and dance about things like that, either building you up as some kind of saint, or writing a lot of hype about rich, idle do-gooders and tarnishing the whole thing, making it look cold and calculated, as if you had taken it on simply to salve your conscience, not because you genuinely cared.

'What time do you want to meet tomorrow night?' she asked quickly. 'And where?'

'Let's have a bite of dinner first. I'll book a table at the Old Vic Restaurant. I'm told they put on a special pre-concert menu, and it's handy to the Concert Hall.'

Her heart sang. 'Shall we meet in the foyer of your hotel, and walk from there?' she suggested, before he could suggest picking her up at her apartment.

'Why not? Six o'clock suit you?'

'Fine. If that's not too early for you. Your conference won't——?'

'No problem. The last session finishes at four-thirty tomorrow, and there's nothing scheduled for the evening. I'm not playing hookey,' he assured her.

'I'm sure you wouldn't,' she said, and meant it. He didn't look the type who would use an overseas conference as an excuse to have a free junket abroad, throwing lectures over to have a good time instead.

Verity had no sooner unlocked her door and stepped into her apartment than her phone rang.

'Hello? Oh, hi, Daddy. Have a good day?' Although his apartment was directly above her own—one of only three apartments in the office tower, the other belonging to her brother Johnny—her father often rang rather than coming down personally. He respected her privacy, while avidly guarding it in other ways.

'Busy, as usual.' She wasn't fooled by that sigh in his voice—her father thrived on work. 'The ballroom looks great, pet—I popped in to have a look. Pleased with it?'

'Very.' She contemplated telling him about Mark, then decided not to. She'd only have to suffer one of her father's famous third degrees. Besides, her father was in a good mood—why spoil it?

'Pet, Gloria and I are having dinner at the Florentino tonight. Want to come with us?'

'Oh, Daddy, you don't want me tagging along!' He was only being fatherly, Verity knew, but he had to realise she was a grown, independent woman now, with her own life to lead, her own friends. 'Look, isn't it about time you made an honest woman of Gloria? You've been squiring her around for—what, two years?' She often worried about her long-widowed father, still on his own after all these years.

'You mean *marry* her?' Lorenzo sounded horrified. 'Never! It would be a disaster—she'd drive me crazy. And vice versa. No, pet, this arrangement is ideal...it suits us both perfectly.'

'You'll end up a lonely old man.'

'Never! There are always other women, if Gloria gets sick and tired of me. Or if I get sick and tired of her. And I have you...and Johnny.'

'You should find someone of your very own, Daddy. Someone permanent, I mean. Someone *special*.' So you can fuss over her, and not me, she mused, sighing.

'There'll never be anyone special for me...not after your mother.' Her father's voice had changed, hardened. 'I'll never marry again—I've told you that a thousand times.'

'Daddy, you've been a widower for twenty-six years...ever since I was a baby. Isn't it about time you——?'

'Verity, I don't *want* to marry again. I don't *need* a wife. No other woman will—can—ever replace your mother. And you needn't start feeling sorry for me,' he warned, his tone lightening. 'When have I ever had to search for a companion? The world is full of luscious widows or divorcees just waiting their chance to comfort an old man.'

'You're not an old man—you're barely sixty-five. And you're very fit and very handsome.' A giant of a man, her father, with thick silver hair and compelling dark eyes. And, heavy as he was, still a mean opponent on the polo field.

'My dear girl, give up, will you? I'm happy with my life as it is—with Gloria or whoever else comes along. And someone else will, I can assure you of that,' he said irrepressibly.

Verity shook her head. 'You're impossible,' she said fondly. Her father had been an incorrigible womaniser for years—just as he had been a bit of a lad, by all accounts, in the years before Verity's mother had burst into his life like a blazing star. That was what Lorenzo had called her—his blazing star—and when he had built up his business as a property developer, diversifying over the years into media networks and entertainment centres, he had adopted the name Star for his conglomerate of companies.

'You *will* join us for dinner?' Lorenzo coaxed.

'Thanks, Daddy, but no, thanks—I'm going to cook myself an omelette and then have an easy night. I want to wash my hair, do my nails, go through my wardrobe... all those female things.'

'Maybe tomorrow night, then—just the two of us?'

'Sorry, Daddy, I'm going to a jazz concert.' Don't ask, she begged silently.

He did. 'With someone special?' he probed, trying— but failing—to sound casual.

'No. No one special.'

'Your voice sounds odd—different. You're not holding out on me, are you?'

'No, Daddy.' Verity drummed her fingers on the desk. 'Someone just had some spare tickets. You'd better go or you'll be late for your dinner. Give my love to Gloria.' She hung up before he could probe any further.

She blew out her breath in a sigh. Her father would have a fit if he knew she was planning to spend an evening with a perfect stranger—a man who had virtually picked her up at the hotel. Or had she picked *him* up? She had a silent chuckle at the thought. That was a first—Verity Danza doing the chasing!

Either way, her father would jump up and down if he knew. He had impressed on her many times how vulnerable the Danzas were—how vulnerable all people of great wealth were. Vulnerable to charlatans, con men, even kidnappers.

He would point out that she only had Mark's word that he was who he said he was. Any con man could pretend to be a noted paediatrician from America. Any con man could have followed her to the ballroom this afternoon.

She found her hand reaching for the phone, dialling the reception desk at the hotel next door.

'Star Hotel. Good evening. May I help you?'

Fortunately, it was a voice she recognised. She wasn't familiar with all the desk staff, but Fiona was a woman she knew well.

'Ah, Fiona—Verity here. Fiona, can you tell me if you have a Dr Mark Bannister staying at the hotel?'

'Dr Bannister? I don't even need to check. He's here all right. In fact, he's giving an address at the medical congress dinner tonight—probably right this minute.'

Verity brightened. Now slow down, she cautioned herself, imagining what her father would be saying at this point. A clever con man could easily claim that *he* was famous Dr Bannister. It would be a brilliant cover.

'Fiona, can you describe him for me?'

She heard a chuckle on the line. 'Can I! He's a real hunk! Stunning grey eyes, brown wavy hair, about six feet two. Strong face, tall, moves like a——' Fiona broke off with a slight cough, as if realising she was getting carried away. 'He's a Yank. Nice voice—deep, resonant, refined, sounds very well educated. His accent's more international, I'd say, than broad American.'

Verity's breath whistled out in relief. 'Thanks, Fiona— I appreciate it. Be seeing you.'

She hung up and gave a whoop of elation. Her charismatic stranger was precisely who and what he had said he was! What was more, there *was* something special about him—even the girl on the desk had sensed it. She would be crazy not to see him again!

Her only sobering thought was that a man so special was bound to have a gorgeous wife waiting for him back home. And if he did, seeing more of him, taking the risk of getting involved... She heaved a deep sigh. Was she making a big mistake?

Despite herself, her heart turned over as she walked into the hotel foyer and saw Mark there waiting for her. She'd had a nagging fear that he wouldn't be, that he'd have changed his mind, that something or someone better might have turned up.

She gave herself a shake. Idiot! He's a James Morrison fan too. The concert's the attraction, not you. He just asked you along out of gratitude, because you did him a good turn and he has nice manners.

'You look great,' he said, his eyes meeting and holding hers for a jolting moment. He couldn't be referring to what she was wearing—he'd barely glanced at her white camisole top and loose suede jacket, or her soft suede skirt. His eyes had zoned straight in on her face... as hers had on his.

*He* looked great too, but she just said hello and gave a warm smile, unaware that her almond-shaped eyes had the brilliance of sapphires and her soft cheeks were glowing in his presence, enhancing the cool beauty of her pale heart-shaped face.

This evening, instead of wearing her black hair in a long glossy mane down her back, as she'd worn it the day before, she had brushed it back behind one ear and swept it round to fall down over her opposite shoulder. She almost gasped as Mark brought his hand up and lightly fingered the lustrous strands, his fingertips just brushing the swell of her breast at the same time.

This man is dynamite, she thought as she tried to still her racing heart, as she tried to find her tongue, and the cool sophistication that in his presence seemed always to desert her.

'Your speech went well at the dinner last night?' she managed, hoping her voice didn't sound as if it had strangled in her throat.

'Seemed to, thanks. How did you pass your day? Why don't you tell me on our way?'

As they left the hotel Verity was acutely conscious of his hand at her elbow, a normal courtesy she would barely have noticed from any other man. Even through the soft suede of her jacket, she was aware of the warmth, the strength of his fingers, aware of delicious tingles, like waves of tiny electric currents, zinging through her veins at his touch.

Outside, dusk was already falling, and a myriad tiny fairy lights twinkled in the plane trees lining Collins Street. She'd seen them before, hundreds of times, but they had never looked more magical. Everything seemed different, more magical tonight—the fresh September air had never seemed so clear and balmy, the old Victorian buildings never more beautiful, the people bustling to and fro more lively or colourful. Maybe she was just seeing Melbourne's most elegant street through Mark's eyes, a stranger's eyes, hoping he would find her city beautiful... beautiful enough to make him want to stay a while longer.

But it wasn't just that, and in her heart she knew it, knew that she was seeing everything this evening with heightened senses because of Mark himself, because he was here with her. And the thought of having him with her for a whole evening excited her most of all.

She gulped down a wave of emotion. What in the world was happening to her? She wasn't an impressionable teenager—she was a twenty-six-year-old sophisticated woman with a broken engagement behind her and a number of other men clamouring for her favours... a woman who, until this point, had always been in full control of her life and her emotions. She was behaving like a wide-eyed young innocent on the brink of...

*No way*, she thought, hardening her heart. She wasn't going down that road again—at least not for a very long time, and not until she was very, very sure of her man.

'Well, now,' Mark said, jolting her out of her foolish thoughts. 'Tell me about your day. You've been at work all day?'

She shook her head. 'Not... exactly.'

He glanced down at her. 'You don't work full-time?'

'No... I'm a freelance designer, you see, and I choose my own hours and the jobs that I take.' She flicked him an anxious glance, realising how arrogant that must sound. He thought so too, she sensed in dismay. She could tell by the way a veil seemed to descend over his eyes, effectively masking his thoughts. In repose, his face looked harder, the lines around his mouth more marked, more cynical.

'And you don't often take on jobs?' he asked, and though his expression was impassive, she sensed a veiled scorn behind the question. Did he think she was just a good-time girl, playing at her job, taking on assignments as the mood took her or when she had nothing better to do... a girl who didn't want her work encroaching on her precious social life, her leisure time? Plenty of people, aware that she was a Danza, had had such thoughts. She knew that, because some had made no secret of it.

But Mark didn't know that she was a Danza. *Did* he? She felt a sudden twinge of doubt.

She wanted to assure him that it wasn't the way it had sounded, that she'd taken on few assignments lately for an entirely different reason ... but how could she without telling him who she was, and what being a Danza, and rich, enabled her to do instead?'

'No, not often,' was all she said, and stifled a sigh, sorely tempted to tell him the truth, wanting him to think well of her. For a second it was on the tip of her tongue to blurt out what she really did with her time... to let him know that because Melbourne had been in deep recession and unemployment was at record levels as a result, she, being a wealthy woman in her own right, had felt it was wrong to take jobs away from other designers who needed the money and the exposure more than she did. Regardless of the fact that she was constantly in demand—her expertise and her flair for design and colour ensured that, and no doubt her name was an added bonus to some—she had knocked back most assignments lately. Not only for that reason, but because she was determined to spend more time on her voluntary work, helping others less fortunate than herself.

Her brief reply, and her ensuing silence, must have convinced Mark that he was right in his assumption, because he changed tack rather abruptly, a hint of derision in the lift of his eyebrow.

'I hope it's a good concert tonight. You go to many shows?' he asked her, a decided reserve in his tone now.

Hearing it, Verity flicked her tongue over her lips. 'Well, since I'm right here in town all week, it's easy for me to get to the theatre, so yes, I do try, when I can, to keep up with the latest plays and films. And I like to go to concerts, and the ballet and the opera too occasionally. I have pretty wide tastes,' she told him with a smile. When he just nodded, she drew in a tremulous breath, again feeling vaguely chastised. Was he starting to see her as a girl who was merely out for a good time?

But I'm not! she wanted to protest. I work damned hard during the day, and deserve some relaxation in the evenings.

'You go out to dinner often?' Mark pursued, eyeing her in a way she couldn't read. 'Parties? Discos?'

She shook her head, answering honestly. 'I'm not crazy about discos, and as for parties...well, it depends on the party and who's going. I do go out to dinner a fair bit—Melbourne has some great pubs and bistros,' she told him, not wanting him to think she frequented exclusive restaurants whenever she went out. He must have realised by now, from what she'd told him, that she wasn't exactly hard up. But she would hate him to think she was simply a social butterfly, one of the idle rich, because nothing could be further from the truth.

'I don't go out every night,' she heard herself adding defensively, though no man before had ever made her feel the necessity to defend herself. Damn him, what *right* had he to make her feel defensive? 'I like to read a lot too—novels, biographies, detective stories, just about anything...don't you?' she said, throwing the pressure back on to him.

'Sure do, especially when I'm travelling, or unwinding after a long day. I was buried in textbooks for so many years that it's good to enjoy a bit of light reading these days, and catch up on the books I wanted to read but missed out on.'

Having found a common interest, they discussed some of the books they'd read, and Verity felt a quiet thrill to find that Mark shared her love for biographies and detective novels, and that he had read quite a few that she had read and loved. They were still locked in a lively exchange of opinions when they arrived at the Arts Centre.

Over their chicken curry and rice in a cosy corner of the Old Vic Restaurant, Mark asked her, 'How's your young friend?'

She looked at him blankly for a second.

'The child you were visiting in hospital,' he prompted, one eyebrow lifting imperceptibly. Was he surprised that she needed reminding? Or was he wondering, perhaps, if the child might be hers? A girl didn't need to wear a ring these days to be a mother. Single mothers were no longer a rarity.

'Oh...yes.' She found herself hesitating, her innate sense of privacy holding her back. But Mark wasn't the media...he wasn't going to spread it around, or beat it up the way the media would. And it wasn't as if he worked for a rival organisation and was pressuring her to come and work for them as well. Some organisations could be very persistent, making impossible demands on her time and on the widely known but unpublicised generosity of the Danza family.

She came to a quick decision. 'I...it wasn't a friend exactly, and it wasn't just one child, it was...several. It's something I do a couple of afternoons a week,' she told him airily. 'I spend a few hours with sick children whose families are unable to come in and visit them. Some families, you see, live a long way away...'

'You mean the hospital employs people to come in and do that?' She saw something glimmer deep in the grey eyes.

'They don't employ me exactly. I do it on a voluntary basis, when I'm needed.' She tilted her chin. 'You look surprised.'

'Not surprised. Impressed.'

'I don't do it to impress people!' She flushed as she heard the sharpness in her voice.

'Sorry. I just meant you're to be commended.' He seemed to withdraw slightly as he said it. Was it because of the sharpness he'd heard in her voice? Or because he didn't want her thinking he *was* all that impressed by her!

'I don't need to be commended either. I do it because...' Verity bit her lip. How could she tell him she did it because she genuinely cared about people, especially people less fortunate than herself... and because her personal wealth allowed her the time to do such things? She didn't want to sound like a sanctimonious do-gooder. 'It's the least I can do.'

'You make it sound as if you owe something to the hospital,' Mark said slowly, trying, obviously, to work her out, to pin down her motives. Though why...? 'Were you once a patient there yourself?' He tilted his head at her.

She laughed. 'No, it's nothing like that. Look, lots of people do voluntary work of one kind or another. Don't they in America?'

'Sure. Sorry, I didn't mean to embarrass you. Another glass of wine?'

'No, thanks. I might go to sleep during the show.' She faced him resolutely. 'I seem to have been talking about myself all evening. Now,' she said firmly, 'it's your turn.'

'OK. Fire away.' He flashed a smile at her, and her heart rolled over at the sight of it, at what it did to his eyes, the fine lines radiating from them, and the cynical lines either side of his mouth. But wasn't there still a faint wariness in the grey depths as well?

'Are you married?' she asked without thinking. Oh, hell, she groaned inwardly, how did that pop out? Now he'll think...

'Divorced,' he said curtly.

Her eyes flickered in surprise. What woman in her right mind would let a man like this out of her clutches? Questions leapt to her lips, but she caught them back. Perhaps, if she were given the chance to get to know him better, to see more of him, she could delve more deeply, then...

'Any children?' was all she asked now.

'No children.' A faint chill in his tone, a tightening of his lips, left her puzzling further. Had he wanted children, perhaps, and his wife hadn't? Had his wife *failed* to have a child, and it had led to friction, and ultimately to a parting of the ways?

There were so many questions she wanted to ask, so much she wanted to know about him!

She changed tack. 'What about your family? Do they live in California too?'

He seemed to pause a moment before answering, his voice sobering as he told her, 'My parents used to live in Texas, not California. They're both dead now. My stepfather died last year, and my mother...just a few months ago.'

'Oh, Mark, I'm sorry. You have brothers? Sisters?'

He shook his head. 'I did have a sister, but she died when she was three years old. When I was eleven.'

Verity caught her breath. 'How terrible! An...accident?'

'No. She had an asthma attack and died before my parents could get her to a hospital.'

'Oh, Mark.' Sympathy raced through her. His baby sister. How awful. She looked at him, light dawning. His own sister, dying of asthma. No wonder he had decided to specialise in childhood asthma!

She gulped back a lump in her throat. 'Is that why you decided to become a paediatrician? Because of your baby sister?'

He nodded. 'I made up my mind at the age of twelve to become a doctor and to specialise—though I didn't know then that it would be in allergy and respiratory diseases. I vowed I'd do everything in my power to ensure that such a thing never happened to another child. I've failed in that,' he conceded sadly, 'but I've never regretted my decision.'

His voice dropped lower, a throb of intensity running through it as he added, 'Since then I've learnt everything there is to know about the disease, and now I'm an authority on the subject, and it's important that I pass on what I know. Too many children die unnecessarily of the disease,' he said grimly. 'People—parents, teachers, medical students, doctors, family doctors in particular—need to know more about it, about how to manage it, about the various treatments, and how to use them properly.'

'And you've offered the medical staff at the Children's Hospital the benefit of your...expertise?'

Mark nodded. 'I'll be visiting other hospitals too, running seminars there, I hope, and doing some lecturing at the university medical schools. And maybe, if I stay here long enough, I'll also visit primary schools and speak to teachers and pupils directly. I'll do whatever I can to educate the people who count.'

'But why here?' Verity asked curiously. 'Why Australia?' And why pick Melbourne in particular? she wondered—glad that he had.

'Because,' he said in all seriousness, 'for some reason Australia has one of the highest incidences of asthma mortality in the world.'

'Really?' She turned shocked eyes to his. 'Why would that be?'

'No one's sure.' He leaned back in his chair. 'But that's not the only reason I've come to Australia,' he admitted.

'It isn't?' She sat very still, sensing a subtle change in the atmosphere, a flickering tension in the air. Was she just imagining it?

'No. I've always wanted to come here.' His hand, barely moving, brushed the air, a mannerism that was as mesmerising as it was distinctively his. 'When I was invited to visit Melbourne as one of the keynote speakers at this paediatrics congress, I jumped at the chance. I've been planning this visit since last year, actually, when the invitation first came. My mother was still alive then, of course, and at that time I was only planning to come for a short visit.'

'But now that she's...' Verity hesitated, not sure how sensitive he was to his mother's death. Was it her memory that had charged the air with that undercurrent of intensity?

He finished for her, his voice a velvet murmur, giving no clue to what he was thinking, let alone feeling. 'Now that she's gone and I have no ties left back in the States, or anywhere else for that matter, I've decided to make it an extended visit. I may even settle out here permanently, make Australia my home,' he said musingly. 'From what I've seen so far, this would be a good place to start afresh, put down roots.'

Verity felt a flutter of breathlessness, her voice husky as she asked, 'You don't have a medical practice to go back to? A house? Relatives? Close friends?'

He shook his head. 'I've sold my practice... sold the house... resigned my post at the university where I was a consultant paediatrician and clinical teacher...and no, I have no relatives, not even distant ones, back in the States, and as for friends—well, friends move on, don't they?'

Verity gulped, studying his face, wishing she could read what lay hidden there as he went on.

'I still own the ranch in Texas that used to be my stepfather's. It's being managed by an excellent young married couple. And I still own the investment company I inherited from him...but I have capable people running that for me too. I'm not saying I'll never go back...naturally I'll need to from time to time. But that's no problem. It might be a long way, but Australia's not the end of the earth.'

Verity's fingers tightened on the cup she was holding. If this fascinating man was thinking of staying in Australia... She hid her delight, a delight tinged with a vague apprehension.

She allowed her soft lips to curve into a smile. 'Well, *we* don't think this is the end of the earth. But a lot of people, Americans in particular, seem to think it is. I guess Australians are *used* to travelling long distances to get anywhere, especially Aussies who live way down south here in Melbourne.'

As a waitress approached, ready to whisk their plates away, Mark glanced at his watch. 'Reckon we have time for more coffee?'

She nodded. 'Plenty of time.' She would have been perfectly content to stay here in the restaurant all night chatting with Mark, learning all she could about him, even if it meant giving James Morrison a miss.

But when they finally left the restaurant and hastened to the Concert Hall next door and settled into their seats, she was soon glad they hadn't missed it.

'He's a genius,' she sighed, happily tapping her feet in time to the beat of the music as the golden strains of

James Morrison's magical trumpet soared to dizzying heights. 'He can play anything, can't he? Trumpet, trombone, piano—you name it. And he's a master of each one.'

She felt Mark's hand on hers, the warmth of his fingers closing over hers, squeezing gently. 'I'm glad you're enjoying it,' he murmured, his head so close to hers that she could feel his breath on her cheek, smell his subtle male fragrance.

I'm enjoying *you* even more, she felt like purring back, aware of an excitement, a zing of anticipation, that she couldn't remember ever experiencing before, not even when she had been making plans to marry Donald.

Did Mark feel the same excitement, the same thrill in *her* company? she wondered, catching his eye for a second, and feeling her breath catch in her throat when she saw an answering spark in the silvery grey of his eyes.

If he does decide to settle in Australia, she found herself wishing, let him settle here in Melbourne. Not in Sydney, not up on the Gold Coast, not over in Perth, not down in Tasmania, but right here... in Melbourne. It would be perfect for him... a good central location for a doctor with a mission. And so wonderfully convenient, she thought... for me!

# CHAPTER THREE

'YOU must tell me more...about yourself,' Mark drawled, his hand protectively on her arm as they dodged the crowd surging across Princes Bridge back to the city. Below them, illuminated by amber floodlights, the old buildings lining the banks of the Yarra cast charming reflections across the water.

Verity felt immensely proud of the way her city looked this evening, and vehemently hoped that Mark would come to love it too in time. If he stayed...

She glanced round at him, trembling as she caught him watching her, feeling a tingling warmth inside at his interest in her, excited by it. How badly she wanted to be able to trust this man! Already she knew quite a bit about him. Surely she could open up, just a little? Mark was man enough, self-sufficient enough in his own right not to be affected by a woman's wealth or background...she was certain of it.

'What would you like to know?' she asked, her soft lips parting in a smile.

He smiled back, and his smile, the fascinating way it tipped up at the edges, was almost her undoing. She found herself tempted to tell him anything...everything!

'Well...' His voice rumbled through her, softly coaxing. 'You haven't told me about your family...or if there's anyone special in your life.'

'There isn't,' she assured him promptly, and flushed, appalled at her eagerness to let him know that she was available—a man she'd only just met! She had never thrown herself at a man before—never needed to, nor wanted to. 'There was someone,' she admitted. But not as special as you, she was tempted to add, despite the fact that at one time she had been on the brink of marrying the man. What an escape!

'We were engaged,' she told him, 'but I broke it off.'

'Mistake, was it?' There was cynicism in his voice now, as if a woman breaking off her engagement came as no surprise to him.

'I found out he'd been deceiving me,' she said, her chin lifting imperceptibly.

He glanced down at her then, not commenting for a moment. Debating, perhaps, whether to probe further? 'You mean... another woman?' he asked at length, as if betrayal was another thing that didn't surprise him.

'Women,' she corrected. 'More than one. Oh, I don't mean just harmless playing around, meeting for drinks, flirting. I mean taking them to bed, the whole bit. I'm glad I found out in time,' she added with a toss of her head. 'I would have hated it if I'd married him and then found out.'

'You say *hated*, not *devastated*.' Mark was eyeing her narrowly. 'You weren't shattered by it, then?' Pinpricks of silver flickered in the smoky eyes.

She shrugged. 'I guess not. It sort of woke me up, to the kind of man he was. To the fact that I didn't love him as much as... well, as much as a girl who's about to marry a man should. So I guess he did me a favour, showing his true colours before it was too late.'

'I guess it's made you a bit wary of men, though, since?' He uttered the words with an ironic twist of his lips. Had he known betrayal himself? she wondered. His wife?

'I suppose I've always been a bit wary of men, even before Donald came along,' she confessed with a sigh. 'It's been drummed into me all my life... that people are not always the way they appear to be.'

'It's not wise to trust anybody these days,' Mark concurred, and she glanced up at him, puzzled by an odd new note in his voice, overriding the cynicism that was still evident. But even in the bright glow of the streetlights his eyes were shadowed, unreadable.

'I think maybe I...don't,' she admitted. But I'd like to know I could trust *you*, she thought, her eyes telling him so.

But Mark's eyes had flicked to the traffic-lights ahead. Steering her across the road, he made no comment until they were safely the other side.

'Tell me...' Only then did he look down at her. 'Who is responsible for making you such a cautious young lady? Your parents?'

'My father, mostly.' She was almost relieved that her father's name had come up at last. If she were to see more of Mark, he would have to know about her father sooner or later. 'My mother died when I was born,' she told him, 'so my father and I have been close all my life. My aunt Elena, Daddy's unmarried sister, helped him to bring me up. And my older brother Johnny, who was nearly three at the time. But she...died last year.'

'I'm sorry. Sudden, was it?' he asked perceptively, his eyes on her face.

She nodded. 'She had a bad fall—she was out riding—and afterwards she suffered a fatal stroke. It came as a terrible shock.'

'I can understand that,' Mark said, his hand brushing over hers. 'You still live with your father? Your brother?'

'Well...sort of. Daddy has an apartment above mine, here in town. And Johnny has the apartment next to mine—only he's overseas at present. I go to Tarmaroo, our place in the country, most weekends—or I try to. Daddy, too, when he's not too busy.'

'But he often *is* too busy? You mean with his work?'

She nodded. 'He thrives on work. Loves it. You could say he's married to it. He swore, after my mother died, that he would never marry again, and he never has. Not that he hasn't had—well...' She gave a quick grin. 'My father likes women,' she said affectionately, with a soft tinkle of laughter. 'He likes their company...oh, one at a time,' she assured Mark quickly, not wanting to give him the wrong impression. 'But, as I said, he's *married* to his work.'

'Must be interesting work...or is that too invasive a question?' Mark's lips eased into a smile, as if to show her that he wouldn't be offended if she preferred not to answer.

'No, not at all.' His smile was disarming her, mesmerising her, dissolving her defences. She paused a moment, casting around for a way to describe her father's huge empire without making a big thing of it. 'He's...well, he's into a lot of different things,' she began, but before she could elaborate Mark intervened.

'I shouldn't have asked,' he said curtly, the muscles of his face stiffening as he shrugged indifferently and glanced away. She looked up at him in dismay. Was he assuming, from her vague answer, that her father must have something to hide, that she was being deliberately evasive because her father was into something...not quite legal?

'Mark, of course you can ask,' she said quickly. 'I was just——'

'It's all right.' Again he cut in, but his tone was softer this time. 'I'm more interested in *you*.' He smiled down at her, his smile dissolving the hardness in his face. 'Do you and your brother Johnny see much of each other?'

She felt a tiny thrill, seduced by the words, '*I'm more interested in you*'. So many men were more interested in her father than in her. Or they just *pretended* to be interested in her, *used* her, to get closer to Lorenzo Danza.

'Well, we're close, but we tend to lead our own lives,' she told him with a smile. 'Johnny's over in America at present doing a business course at Harvard. He works for my father... he'll be taking over the family business one day.' There, if he really wants to know, she thought, I've given him another opening. She held her breath, fully expecting the questions to come.

They didn't, surprising her anew. Disarming her anew.

'Where's your apartment?' Mark asked as they turned into Collins Street. 'I'll walk you home.'

'Thanks, but there's no need,' she said, smiling to soften her refusal. 'It's only a few steps from the hotel where you're staying.'

'From the Star?' He looked surprised. Few people lived, or could afford to live, right here in the heart of the city. 'Even so, I'll still walk you home. Back in the States, a guy sees a girl to her door. It's not safe for a girl to wander about the city streets alone at night.'

'I won't be wandering around the streets at night. I told you, it's——'

'What's the matter, Verity?' He swung round to face her, his eyes seeking hers, holding them. 'Don't you trust me enough to see you home?'

She saw amusement, a hint of challenge, rather than pique, shimmering in the grey depths. 'Of course I do.' And she did, she realised. Was that foolishly naïve of her? 'It's not that,' she assured him. 'It's just that— well, it's not necessary, that's all.' She came to a sudden decision. 'You see, the Star Hotel, where you're staying— it's part of the Star Tower complex, as you must know. The twin towers are linked by a covered space, with shops at ground level. One tower is the hotel, the other an office building.'

He nodded, looking faintly mystified.

'Well, my apartment is in the office tower—Star Tower,' she told him lightly. 'It's mostly offices, but there's a gym too, and apartments on the upper floors.' No need at this point to tell him there were only three private apartments, all owned and lived in by the Danza family. 'So you see, I won't be out wandering the streets!'

'Aha,' he said, and for a second she thought that was all he was going to say. Then, 'I'll see you to your door all the same... and I assure you,' he added with an easy smile, 'I won't expect you to ask me in.'

'Oh, Mark, that's not what I'm——' She broke off, feeling foolish now for being so evasive, so over-cautious, so... stupidly apprehensive. It was all very well to be wary of men, and take natural precautions. But Mark wasn't just any man. It was ridiculous trying to keep him away from her apartment simply because she didn't want him seeing the luxury in which she lived, for fear he'd get the wrong idea about her. If Mark was the type who judged a girl by the manner in which she lived, by the shallow trappings of wealth, then he wasn't the man she thought he was, the man she was beginning to know and admire—emotions entirely aside.

'I'd be pleased if you would see me home,' she accepted, smiling back at him. 'Thank you.'

'My pleasure,' he said, and her ears, attuned to lecherous overtones from men, heard nothing but quiet sincerity in his voice, and the eyes that met hers were reassuringly bland.

They talked of other things as they strolled up Collins Street, arriving at the Star Towers almost too soon for Verity's liking. She let herself into the glass-fronted office building with her own special pass key, nodding to the security man as they passed by his desk on their way to the lifts, their heels clicking on the highly polished marble floor, their voices, hushed though they were, echoing from wall to wall in the bare, cavernous lobby.

The Danza family had their own private lift. Verity used her security key to gain access to it, pushing the button to send it to the second to top floor, where her apartment and Johnny's were situated side by side. Her father's luxurious penthouse apartment was directly above, taking up the whole of the top floor.

As they rode up, Mark asked, 'Do you realise I still don't know your full name? It might be an idea to let me know what it is,' he invited, cocking an eyebrow at her, 'if we're to meet again some time.'

Did that mean... he *wanted* to see her again? Verity drew in a tremulous breath, trying to calm the accelerated beat of her heart. '*If*', he'd said. And '*some time*'... She bit her lip in sudden doubt. He made it sound so vague, so indefinite. I don't want you slipping out of my life, Mark Bannister, she realised as the lift came to a silent halt at her floor.

'Verity Danza,' she told him lightly as they stepped from the lift into the elegant cream and gold hallway.

'Danza?' He repeated the name, his brow puckering, as if he'd heard it before somewhere. Or was he simply wondering... 'Italian?' he asked, confirming her second thought.

She nodded. 'That is, my grandparents were Italian. My parents were both born here in Australia. My mother had Italian blood too, on her father's side.'

'You don't look Italian.' He tilted his head at her. 'I guess it's the blue eyes... such a deep blue, verging on violet.' As his gaze held hers she was acutely aware of the tiny silver flecks in the deep grey of his own eyes. 'Not that all Italians have brown eyes... I realise that. Mind you,' he added gallantly, 'with that stunning black hair and willowy figure, and the way you move and dress, you have the style and grace that Italian women are famous for.'

## SHATTERED WEDDING 43

'Well, thank you.' Used as she was to elaborate compliments, hearing them now from Mark seemed somehow quite different... fresh, special, bringing a swift flush to her cheeks, which in turn brought a new radiance, a warm translucent glow, to her smooth olive skin, though she herself was unaware of it.

'I take after my mother, I'm told. Daddy says I'm the image of her.' She was digging into her handbag for her key as she spoke, trying as she did so to regain her poise.

'I see why you weren't too concerned about coming home by yourself,' Mark commented, wry amusement in his tone. 'With all this security you wouldn't need to be.'

She glanced up at him, briefly searching his face. He must be wondering why such elaborate security was needed for a simple country girl who spent only her working week in the city.

'Daddy's a stickler for security,' she said with a shrug. 'He tends to be over-protective, which I find rather stifling—and irritating at times. But I guess it's wise... you hear of some pretty hairy things happening to women these days.'

As she found her key and thrust it into the door of her apartment, she turned her head and said, 'Mark, I'd *like* you to come in for coffee.' The invitation had popped out involuntarily but she meant it none the less. She wanted him to know that she didn't see him as she did other men, as someone a girl needed to watch closely and be ultra-wary of. She wanted him to feel that she trusted him—even if deep down a part of her wasn't quite sure of him yet. Her father, she mused at the same time, would think her mad, inviting a man she barely knew into her apartment, taking a stranger on trust. Well, too bad, she thought recklessly. He needn't know!

'Well, now... I don't know,' Mark demurred. 'It's getting late. I don't want to disturb your family...'

'You won't be. Daddy's apartment is up above, quite separate from mine.' Verity pushed open her door and switched on the soft wall lights, illuminating the spacious ultra-modern interior. 'Please, Mark, do come in. Just for a moment.'

'Well, since you insist.' As he stepped inside and followed her through the flower-scented hall into the vast lounge-dining area, with its high ornate ceiling and soft pastel furnishings and leafy indoor plants, he whistled. 'Very nice. There's obviously good money in interior design,' he added, his lip quirking.

She gave a careless laugh. 'Not this good, I'm afraid. It's really my father who...' She hesitated a moment, then admitted reluctantly, 'He owns this building.' She bit her lip, heaving a faint sigh as she went on to explain, 'He's a property developer—among other things. He owns the Star Group of companies,' she told him, knowing he would have to know some time. And as she had already told him her father's name, he could easily have found out from someone else. Best, perhaps, that it should come from her, from someone who wouldn't embellish it, make a big thing of it.

'Ah...' Mark said slowly. 'The Star Group...the Star Towers complex...' He stared at her. 'You're saying your father owns the whole complex—including the hotel where I'm staying?' He grimaced as she nodded. 'Oh, hell. You must have had a silent chuckle when I took you for the florist!'

She smiled, and shook her head. 'I thought it was great. I'd rather people *didn't* know that I'm a Danza,' she confessed.

'No? Why?' He turned slowly to face her. 'You mean you're ashamed to be a Danza? People point a finger at the Danzas for some reason?'

Was he implying that the Danzas might have made their money dishonestly?

'Heavens, no, it's nothing like that.' She drew in a deep breath as she moved over to her compact disc player. As Sarah Vaughan's glorious voice soared into the air, she turned her head to see Mark strolling round the room, inspecting the Australian oil-paintings and watercolours adorning the walls, the pieces of pottery and porcelain she'd acquired over the years, the soft leather furnishings.

'You're not...comfortable with all this?' he asked, swinging round to face her.

Verity's brow puckered. 'What do you mean?'

'You didn't want me to know, did you, that you live in such luxury, that your family is...well, obviously very well off? You kept it from me for as long as you could. Why?' he asked softly, his eyes holding hers so that she couldn't escape the smoky, compelling gaze. 'Because you were afraid I might be a fortune-hunter? Or are you uneasy about having all this wealth because you feel it's come too easily, that your family, perhaps, hasn't earned it the hard way?'

For a second she didn't know what to say, how to answer, his directness disconcerting her. But his tone was not disparaging. It was almost sympathetic. It was impossible to take offence.

'I wouldn't say it's come easily at all,' she said slowly. 'My father's worked very hard for what he now has. He's a self-made man,' she asserted proudly. 'He began with nothing. When he started out he was just a labourer, pouring concrete... barely making a living.'

'And he's acquired all this, through sheer hard work?' Mark made a sweep of his hand, but she knew he wasn't referring only to her apartment. He meant the whole complex, the entire Star Group of companies.

A faint frown flitted across her brow. 'Are you implying something?' Her heart was sinking as she asked the question. She had been so sure that Mark wouldn't care about her background, wouldn't be affected by it, wouldn't let her obvious wealth taint their relationship. Relationship? A bit early to be thinking in those terms, she chided herself.

He answered with a soft laugh, 'No, not at all. Why...have other people? You sound a trifle defensive.'

'I'm not being defensive. I'm just surprised, that's all.' She looked Mark straight in the eye. 'Nobody has ever pointed an accusing finger at my father. Not ever. He has a spotless reputation...there's never been anything to point a finger *at*.'

'Verity, forgive me, please. I didn't mean to upset you. You took me the wrong way.'

'Sorry. I...' She floundered under the brilliance of his gaze. Maybe she *had* over-reacted, jumped to conclusions. She did tend to be a bit prickly and defensive, she guessed, where her family was concerned. Stay cool, you idiot, or Mark will walk straight out of the door! She flashed a smile. 'Mark, would you like to sit down? I'll just go and put the coffee on.'

'I'll come and help,' he said, and giving her no chance to refuse his offer, followed her through to the compact kitchen.

As she prepared the coffee and reached into the cupboard for two mugs, Mark said admiringly,

'How do you keep this place so spotless? You wouldn't have time, surely, to...' He paused, an eyebrow shooting up, the cynical lines round his mouth deepening. 'Of course, you'd have staff laid on.'

Verity flushed. 'We have this wonderful woman, Frederica, who comes in each day to clean and tidy and make sure we have food in the pantry. She'll prepare meals too if we want her to.'

'Sounds a gem,' he said before asking casually, 'You normally eat together...you and your father?'

'Well, no, not that often, actually. We don't live in each other's pockets.' She tilted her chin. 'In fact, I'm thinking of moving out of here soon, finding somewhere smaller and—well, easier for my friends to come and go,' she said, avoiding his eye as she placed the cups on the bench.

'You have a lot of friends here in Melbourne?' Mark asked.

She turned, eyeing him speculatively from under her sweeping lashes. Did he think she was a poor lonely little rich girl? 'Yes, quite a few,' she said.

'Female and male, I take it?' His grey eyes glinted at her.

'Female mostly... since Donald,' she said, gulping as she heard the faint huskiness in her voice, and knowing that it was nothing to do with Donald, it was because of this man... this tantalising, fascinating stranger who had burst so suddenly into her life.

Suddenly she felt the air pressing in on her, felt the muscles of her body tensing in acute awareness as she realised how close, physically, he was, and how confined they both were, all alone here in her small silent kitchen.

She moistened her lips with the tip of her tongue, and swallowed as she felt his eyes on her mouth. She could feel her cheeks burning under his smouldering gaze. Oh, this is crazy, she thought wildly. I'm never nervous with men... why *now*?

In her panic she swung round, away from him, grabbing the handle of the coffee-pot almost like a lifeline as she fought for her usual composure.

'Milk? Sugar?' she mumbled as she dashed hot coffee into the two mugs.

'One sugar, no milk.' She heard the thread of amusement in his voice and felt like kicking herself. She was behaving like a nervous schoolgirl!

Mortified, she tossed in the sugar, spilling a few grains in her haste. 'Biscuit?' she croaked, and without waiting for an answer, reached up to grab the biscuit tin from the cupboard above. She felt his hand touch her arm and a tremor shuddered through her.

'Just coffee, thanks. Here, let me carry them.' Had he noticed that her hands were shaking? Summoning all her powers of self-control, she stood meekly aside while Mark scooped up the two cups from the bench and carrying one in each hand, brushed past her, heading back to the lounge.

'Just put them down here.' She waved to a low coffee table. 'Make yourself comfortable.' She turned away to change the compact disc, heaving a deep sigh as she put on some soft mood music, soothing to the nerves. Then, dropping into the armchair opposite his, she fended off more questions by tossing one at him.

'Your accent, Mark...isn't there a touch of—an English accent there?'

'So it's still evident, is it? Well, not surprising. I was brought up in England. But I left there when I was twelve, around the time my mother married my stepfather—a widower from Texas. He was touring England when they met, and she was a guide on his tour bus. Within weeks he'd asked her to marry him, and he brought us back to the States with him, to his ranch in Texas.'

'Oh, so your mother was——'

'English, yes.' Mark raised his coffee-cup to his lips and swallowed deeply. 'My stepfather, Sam, was a great guy. He had no children of his own, and treated me like a real son.'

'And your father? Is he——?'

'Still alive? I wouldn't know...we lost touch a long time ago.' His mouth twisted in a faint grimace. 'He ran off with another woman when I was eleven—that's why my mother divorced him.'

'And he's never tried to see you again? His own son?'

Mark shook his head. 'We were never close. My little sister Katy was his favourite—he doted on her. After she died he lost interest in me altogether. Lost interest in my mother too. He was devastated when Katy died.'

'But surely your mother was too? And you too...so much so that you've devoted yourself to medicine as a result!' Verity's cheeks glowed with indignation. How could a father, a husband, be so self-centred, so insensitive to the needs, the suffering of his family?

'I guess we all show our grief in different ways,' Mark said without apparent emotion. 'My father just went to pieces. Instead of it bringing him closer to my mother, he turned away from her—from both of us.'

Verity's eyes darkened with compassion. 'You'd think, after losing one child, his other would become more precious.'

'It doesn't always work like that.' Mark drained the rest of his coffee. 'Don't feel sorry for me, Verity. I can't say I've ever missed him. My stepfather more than made up for any loss. He taught me a lot, gave me every opportunity in life. He had the means to do it,' he added with a quirk of his lip. 'He'd made his fortune from oil, and had invested it wisely. It just grew and grew. After he died, the fortune he'd built up came to my mother, and in turn to me.'

As he paused, she smiled at him. So he was wealthy too...extremely wealthy, obviously. She felt a weight slide from her shoulders. He couldn't be a fortune-hunter. Not that she'd ever thought——

'Great wealth, I find, makes life both harder...and easier,' Mark said musingly. 'Does your family's wealth ever bother you, Verity?' he asked, reaching out to set his cup down on the table.

'Bother me?' She hesitated. 'Not in itself, no. It bothers me more when other people are affected by it, when it affects their perception of me, or my family. We try not to flaunt our wealth. We *don't* flaunt it.' She flushed as she saw Mark's gaze flicker around the room, but he made no comment. 'We're very private people,' she asserted. 'We like to keep to ourselves. We despise personal publicity, making a big splash in public. For instance, my father gives very generously to numerous charities, but he does it quietly... he won't have it publicised.'

'Very commendable. While having its tax advantages, I dare say.' Mark's eyebrows rose a fraction.

'Well, it may, I guess, but that's not why——'

'Of course not,' he broke in smoothly. 'People do tend to jump to conclusions, I find, where a lot of money is involved.' He sighed, as if he'd had that same problem. 'You're damned if you splash it around, and you're damned if you keep it hidden, under wraps.'

'What... do you mean?'

'Well, you tell me your family tend to be low-key. You don't shout about your wealth or about what you do with it...' He spread his hands as she nodded. 'From my experience, there'll always be people who'll seize on that and say you must have something to hide, that you must have acquired it in some dubious way...' He paused, grimacing. 'One of the burdens of wealth, I guess.'

He seemed to be watching her, waiting for something... to see if she agreed?

'I must say my family have been lucky that way,' she said slowly. 'Nobody's ever spread any evil stories like that about us. As far as I know, there have never even been any snide whispers. I think, if you're honest and sincere and above board, you're not giving people any fuel to start with, and that's what leads to rumours.'

'From my experience, rumours, unfortunately, *can* start from nothing, or at least from very little,' Mark said, his brow lowering. 'For instance, people try to minimise their tax, but it doesn't mean they're blatantly *evading* tax. But sometimes there's a fine line...it's not always clear.' He shrugged. 'It's the same with crime. Crimes can be seen in different ways, to different people. They become a matter of degree, in some people's eyes.'

Verity looked at him, startled. 'Is that how you feel, Mark?' Disappointment swept through her. 'That certain shades of crime...and some degree of tax evasion...are acceptable?'

He gave a hint of a smile, not answering directly. 'You don't feel that way?'

'No, I don't! And neither does my father,' she cried hotly. 'Just because some people make their fortunes that way, it doesn't mean that all wealthy people do. Is it different in America, Mark? Are you all a bit...shady over there? Are *you*?'

He gave a soft laugh, and held up his hand. 'Not guilty, I promise you. And I wasn't insinuating... Hell, I've made a proper mess of this, haven't I? I didn't mean to upset you, Verity, or to imply... Damn!' He caught her gaze with his, his grey eyes darkening in genuine remorse. 'Forgive me?'

She felt weak under his gaze. 'Of course I do,' she said without hesitation, relief coursing through her. Mark had just wanted to make sure, to reassure himself that she—that the Danza family—were as squeaky-clean as he was himself. It was perfectly understandable that he would want to know if there was anything—well, dubious in her background before he committed himself to seeing more of her, let alone allowed himself to get more deeply involved with her—or her family.

'You see what the subject of money can do to people?' Mark sighed. 'Great wealth...it brings a lot of problems... and a lot of power,' he said slowly, his eyes on hers.

Verity nodded thoughtfully. 'Yes, I guess great wealth can be used... for good or for evil.' As the words came out she laughed self-consciously. She didn't want him thinking her a prude, or a pious do-gooder.

'Oh, don't get me wrong,' Mark said swiftly. 'I don't regret my sudden windfall. I'm not about to squander it all on riotous living, or throw it away to a dogs' home, just to get rid of it. I intend to put it to good use.'

Something in his voice made her shiver, she wasn't sure why. The eyes holding hers were narrowed, unfathomable. They seemed to be looking right through her now, *beyond* her.

'In... what way?' she ventured huskily.

His eyelids flickered under her gaze. 'Oh, there are various projects I have in mind...' He paused, seeming reluctant to spell them out. 'Some personal, some to do with my work. I'll find some deserving charities as well... and not,' he added drily, 'merely for tax advantages.' He glanced at his watch. 'Hell, look at the time!' He rose, unfolding his lithe frame with tigerish grace. 'I've outstayed my welcome. I must let you get some sleep.'

Verity jumped up too, aware of a low thudding in her chest. Would he want to see her again?

'You have a busy day at your conference tomorrow?' she asked as she escorted him to the door.

'Full to the hilt. With a lunch thrown in and another session in the evening after dinner.'

She felt her spirits dip. *'Full to the hilt'*... Was that true? Or just an excuse?

'What about you? Busy day tomorrow?' he asked, pausing at the door, his hand hovering, hypnotically, in mid-air.

She nodded. 'I've some work to do in the morning, and a bit of running around in the afternoon.' Nothing she couldn't have changed if Mark had been available and had wanted to meet her.

'Interior design work?' he hazarded. 'Another hospital visit?'

'No, just——'

'Just a game of bridge with the girls?' he broke in teasingly. 'Hairdresser? Shopping? A workout in the gym?'

She flushed. 'I don't play bridge, I do my own hair, and I only shop when I particularly need something—I'm not a compulsive shopper by any means. And I get enough exercise just by rushing around.' She was finding it hard to breathe with Mark standing so close. She had never felt so tense, so nervy, wondering if he would want to see her again, or if this was the last she would ever see of him.

'Sorry. Just joking.' He didn't press her, or give her a chance to elaborate about what she did do. 'Look, I must go. May I call you again?' he asked. His tone was impassive now, coolly polite, and when she looked up at him she noted a tightness about his mouth, sensed a faint aloofness. It shook her for a second, until his words sank in. Surely he wouldn't be asking unless...

A smile burst from her lips. For a second she was unable to speak, relief sweeping over her. He did want to see her again! If he seemed aloof, it was because he was feeling as tense as she...bracing himself, perhaps, for a refusal?

'I'd like that,' she managed at last, her voice faint, husky, unlike her own. She gulped, and twisted round, snatching up her handbag and burying her hand deep inside. 'Here...my phone number's on this card.'

He took it from her and slipped it into his pocket with barely a glance. 'Goodnight, Verity.' He swayed over her, his face a mere breath away, their bodies almost touching. She caught her breath, feeling the tension inside her throbbing, building in her lungs.

'Thank you, Mark, for a wonderful evening,' she almost gasped. She wasn't thinking of the jazz concert, which seemed a hazy memory already. She was thinking of him, only of him...of seeing him again, and, wonder of wonders, of him wanting to see more of her. Was she being a gullible fool? Leaving herself open to more disillusionment, more hurt? It could be real hurt this time, she suspected...a hurt that could go deep, crush her. Would he turn out to be another Donald...another heartless womaniser?

'It's only whetted my appetite for more evenings,' Mark said gallantly, his face blurring above hers, the silvery pools of his eyes seeming to swallow her own.

Almost against her will, Verity tilted her chin, expectancy in her eyes, wanting him to kiss her, *inviting* him to. Most men who took her out for an evening expected a goodnight kiss as their due, and in the past she had either reluctantly submitted or shown them the door. She had never before actively *sought* a man's kiss.

The air seemed to crackle and pulsate between them for a long endless second. She could feel Mark's warm breath on her face, was dimly aware of his eyes shining like buffed silver above hers. She saw his lips part, and, breathless, she waited, her lungs straining for air. He whispered, 'I've enjoyed it,' and in the next instant, before she could even blink, he was gone, leaving a faint chill in the air where he had been, the sound of the door shutting behind him the only sound he made.

She staggered sideways, leaning against the closed door for support, her hand fluttering up to touch her lips. He hadn't kissed her, hadn't even brushed her lips with his, and yet...and yet she felt as shaken as if he had swept her into a passionate embrace and crushed his mouth savagely down on hers.

After a long stunned moment she stumbled into her bedroom, sinking down on the stool in front of her dressing-table and gazing, still dazed, into the mirror. She let out a sigh, hardly recognising her own reflection, the quivering mouth, the glowing cheeks, the over-bright eyes, their usual deep blue now a dark glittering violet.

She had never felt like this before in her life, so shaken, so aware of a man, so painfully vulnerable, or so...alive. Or so anxious, she acknowledged with another deep sigh. It was rather scary, feeling the way she was starting to feel about Mark, a man she'd only just met and barely knew anything about. It didn't happen like this, it couldn't—not so quickly, so dramatically...

*Could* it?

What precisely did she know about him? Sure, he'd talked about his work, his family, the tragedy of his baby sister, his inheritance... but what else did she know? He was divorced, but that was all he'd told her about his marriage. She knew nothing about how the break-up of his marriage had affected him, how long he and his wife had been together, or if he still had feelings, unresolved or otherwise, for his ex-wife, or even if he was still in contact with her. He might have other hang-ups, other skeletons in his closet, for all she knew. Anything could come to light to shatter the wonder, the excitement she felt when she was with him. Anything could happen to pour cold water on her newly awakening feelings...

If anything did, she didn't think she could bear it.

## CHAPTER FOUR

HER phone was ringing as she unlocked the door of her apartment the next day. Dashing inside, she grabbed it before the answering machine took over.

'Verity, where have you been?' She felt a swift stab of disappointment when she heard her father's voice. Resentment swiftly followed. What right had he to question her?

'I've been at the therapy centre all afternoon,' she almost snapped at him. 'I've only just walked in. And this morning—not that it's any business of yours, Daddy—I had to deliver some toys to one of the branches. The toy library——'

Her father cut in, not interested in the details. 'You'll wear yourself out doing all this voluntary work you do. Why can't you just give a donation, or help with fund-raising?'

She sighed. 'The Danza family already give massive donations,' she reminded him, 'and there are plenty of people more interested in fund-raising than I am—and better at it. What these organisations need is people with time and energy and wheels, and a willingness to do any kind of work.'

'Well, just don't let it all get on top of you. When did you last take a break?'

'Daddy, I go home nearly every weekend. What could be more relaxing than that?'

'A weekend at Tarmaroo!' He snorted. 'Half the time you take work with you...'

'Not for a while. I haven't been taking on much interior design work lately, remember.'

'It defeats me why not. You're so damned good at it...'

'Daddy, you know why, I've told you a——'

'OK, OK, don't let's fight. This has been a good day for me and I want to celebrate with my favourite girl. You haven't had dinner yet?'

'Not yet, I've only just——'

'We'll go to the Zodiac Room at the hotel. I like them to see me there occasionally... it keeps the staff on their toes. You haven't made any other plans?'

He sounded so anxious for her company that she backed down, assuring him quickly, 'No, none. The Zodiac Room sounds fine. What time?'

'Pick you up in half an hour.'

'Fine.' Just time to freshen up and change, and play back the messages on her answering phone to see if Mark had called yet. She knew *he* wouldn't be asking her out tonight—he'd told her last night that he would be tied up with the conference people all evening. But maybe he had something in mind for tomorrow...

She heaved a sigh when there was no message from him. It rather dampened her spirits, but she put on a bright face when her father knocked at her door.

'Ready?'

'I'm ready.' She gave him a smile, flicking fond eyes over his huge frame, the thick mane of silver hair, the intense brown eyes. Lorenzo Danza looked tough and powerful, and he was. But he had a softer side that he reserved for his family and closest friends and the most loyal of his staff, and, despite her aggravation when he interfered in her life, she loved him dearly.

'You look nice.' He bent to kiss her. 'New dress?'

She laughed. 'You've seen it before.' He never remembered. He always thought she looked nice, no matter what she wore. And he always liked her in blue, the colour he said suited her best, enhancing the blue of her eyes and the rich ebony sheen of her hair.

As they rode down in the lift and strolled across to the Star Hotel, Verity said, 'You seem in a good mood, Daddy. What happened today? Shares gone up? Swung a big business deal? Found a fabulous new site to build on?' Her eyes were teasing.

'It's better than that—far better. It's my casino bid. It's looking more promising by the day. I have a feeling, my pet, that we're going to win!'

'Oh, Daddy, that's great!' She knew how badly her father wanted this project. It had been his dream for a long time to build Melbourne's first casino. When the Government, after years of vacillating, had finally called for registrations of interest, her father had had his proposal all prepared, ready to send in. As he'd expected, he had reached the short-list, and along with a handful of other hopefuls had since lodged a detailed formal submission.

'Well?' she asked as they caught a lift to the elegant Zodiac Room, 'what have you heard to make you feel so confident?'

'Whispers,' her father said mysteriously. 'You know how these things leak out. They're saying my submission is so good it's bound to be chosen.'

'What about the Hammond Group up in Sydney...the ones who built those fabulous resorts along the coast? You've always said they're likely to be your most dangerous rival.'

She remembered how Jack Hammond had boasted in the Press a couple of years ago that his development and construction company had already drawn up plans for a Melbourne casino...a revolutionary design that would put Queensland's Jupiter's Casino in the shade and even rival the design of Sydney's fabulous Opera House, putting Melbourne on the world map. It had had a lot of publicity at the time, and her father had always considered Hammond his greatest threat.

Lorenzo chuckled. 'There's a hot rumour that Hammond will have to pull out of the race. Apparently his business is in big trouble financially.'

'You're kidding! Bad enough to have to pull out?'

'Looks that way.' He beamed down at her. 'They've been over-extending themselves for years,' he said with cheerful satisfaction. 'They've borrowed far too much in recent years, expanded too quickly, and now, as a result of the recession—and their greed—they're struggling to survive. Oh, they've been desperately trying to cover it up, to find a way out of the mess they're in, but Hammond's going under all right. A Sydney contact of mine heard one of the Hammond directors admit it, only last week. I would have expected an announcement by now.'

'Wow. Well, that's good news, Daddy...for you.'

Lorenzo shook his head indulgently at her. Her compassion always mystified him. 'Don't feel sorry for them, pet. They don't deserve it. They've been too grasping, too carried away by their insane greed to acquire more and more property and make a dazzling impression... and now they're paying for it.'

They both fell silent as they reached the glass doors of the restaurant. The *maître d'* hastened over to greet them.

'Mr Danza! And you've brought your lovely daughter! Good to see you both again. Let me show you to your table.'

'Lead the way, Stefan,' Lorenzo said genially. As they wended their way through the softly lit restaurant, heading for their special table in the far corner, he paused, touching Verity's arm.

'Well, there's Frank...Dr Richards. Remember him, pet? He was one of the doctors who bought that private hospital we built a couple of years ago. You did the interior design.'

'Oh, yes, I remember,' Verity said, and as she glanced round she caught her breath, her heart skipping in mingled joy and panic. Dr Richards she had recognised at once, but now, as her gaze flickered to the doctor's male companion, she saw that it was Mark. He was deep in conversation, his strong profile intent on the man opposite.

Lorenzo was already making a beeline for Dr Richards's table, sweeping Verity along with him. She was in an agony of suspense, her legs feeling stiff as she moved. Would Mark be pleased to see her again? He hadn't called...but then he'd been tied up all day and it was only last night, after all, that he'd asked if he could call her.

Clenching her hands into tight little fists, she tried to regain her normal cool composure as both men broke off their conversation and turned their heads at their approach.

'Lorenzo! Verity, my dear!' As Frank Richards, smiling broadly, rose from his chair, Mark rose too, his grey eyes flicking from Lorenzo's tall lumbering frame to the slender figure at his side. As Mark's eyes met hers, Verity saw warmth flicker in the cool grey depths and her heart turned over, her lips bursting into a smile.

'Good to see you both.' Frank Richards was extending his hand to her father. 'Lorenzo, let me introduce a colleague of mine... Dr Mark Bannister, who's come all the way from America to speak at our conference. Mark, I'd like you to meet——'

'Good evening, Miss Danza,' Mark was saying at the same time. He was smiling at Verity, his charm flowing over her as he acknowledged that they had already met. 'Good to see you again.'

'Good evening, Dr Bannister,' Verity said with equal politeness, but the radiance of her smile and the deep sapphire glow of her eyes belied the formality of her greeting. 'It's good to see you too.'

'Well, I see you two have already met,' Frank said, and Verity, catching her father's enquiring look, said hastily, 'We've met a couple of times, actually. Mark, I'd like you to meet my father, Lorenzo Danza.'

As the two men solemnly shook hands, Verity was conscious of them sizing each other up. Her father had sensed her interest in Mark—if only she had managed to hide it better!—and, as she knew only too well, any man who caught her interest earned close scrutiny by her father!

'Mark is an authority on children's asthma, Daddy,' she added quickly, anxious for him to think well of Mark, and at the same time hoping to divert him from more personal questions. 'The Children's Hospital have asked him to do some work for them after the conference.' Let him think that was where they had met.

'You intend to extend your stay in Australia for a while?' Lorenzo asked Mark. His tone was pleasant enough, but Verity, knowing him as she did, knew that he hadn't asked simply out of politeness—he wanted to know what Mark's intentions were, while at the same time subtly warning his daughter that her doctor friend was unlikely to be in their country for long. *'Your stay'*, he'd said, and *'for a while'*... reminding her that Mark was merely a visitor to their shores and wouldn't be here for long.

'I'll be staying for some time, I hope,' Mark said, the arrogant tilt of his jaw indicating that he didn't intend to be awed by her father. 'I have long-term plans here. But they'll depend, of course, on...a number of factors,' he said enigmatically. He didn't even glance at Verity as he said it, and she wasn't sure whether to feel relieved or downcast. Was she just imagining it, or was there an edge to Mark's voice, his tone almost... challenging?

'I'd invite you to join us,' Frank intervened, his tone apologetic, 'but we've already had our dinner...' He waved his hand at the empty coffee-cups on the table. 'We have to leave in a few minutes... we're both involved in tonight's seminar.'

'And Stefan's waiting to take us to our table,' said Lorenzo. 'Hospital going OK, Frank?' he asked as they prepared to take their leave.

'Fine, just fine.'

'Good. I must drop out there some time. Enjoy your stay, Dr Bannister. I hope you won't find your work schedule in Australia too demanding in the time you're here. Coming, my dear?'

Verity barely had time to bid the two men goodnight before her father, catching her arm, propelled her away.

Her cheeks were still flushed as they settled down at their table in a quiet alcove, but this time her high colour was not so much from elation at seeing Mark again as from vexation at her father's negative reaction to Mark.

'OK, Daddy, what's wrong?' she demanded. 'You were warning me off. Why? Because Mark's an American? A foreigner?'

'Of course not... though it might be an idea to keep that in mind. He won't stay in Australia, not for long. Why should he, if he's such a hot-shot in the American medical world? I don't want to see my daughter running off to the States to live. I don't want to lose you,' he said gruffly.

'Oh, Daddy, you'll never lose me, no matter where I end up living.' She curbed her exasperation, knowing Lorenzo felt doubly responsible for her now that Aunt Elena, the only mother she had ever known, had gone.

'Not that I have any no intention of leaving Australia, I assure you... and as for marrying Dr Mark Bannister, whether he decides to stay in Australia or not... Well, you're being ridiculous, Daddy. I've only just met him.'

'I fell in love with your mother at first sight,' her father reminded her glumly. 'I know it can happen.'

'Daddy, hadn't we better order?' she said hastily, her eyes flicking to the waitress standing by.

Silence reigned as they made their selections, and as they waited for their first course Verity tried to divert her father by asking about his casino bid. But his answers were short, preoccupied, and finally he cut off her questions altogether, demanding abruptly, 'How do you know the man isn't married?'

She sighed. No point pretending she didn't know who he was talking about. 'He isn't. He's... divorced.'

Involuntarily, her gaze flickered round, just in time to see Mark and Frank Richards leaving the restaurant, only their retreating backs visible. A tiny piece of herself left with them.

'Divorced!' Her father spat out the word, his tone saying, *I might have guessed*. 'I'd want to know why his wife divorced him, if I were you. He could be the type who plays around... who beats his wife...'

'Oh, Daddy, *please*! All men aren't monsters, or womanisers like Donald. Maybe Mark divorced *her*. Or maybe it was a mutual parting of the ways. People aren't always suited to each other, you know.'

'If a man truly loves a woman, it's for life,' Lorenzo said doggedly. 'If your mother had lived I would never have looked at another woman. Even after all this time, no other woman can compare...' He cleared his throat. 'Why do you think I've never remarried?'

'Daddy, everyone's not as lucky as you were with my mother,' Verity said gently. 'And you only had a short time together... barely four years. Who's to say you wouldn't have grown apart one day if——'

'Never! We were twin souls, your mother and I. Our love was unbreakable. It would have lasted forever. That's what I want to see for you, Verity, a love that will last a lifetime. So don't you go setting your cap at this Dr Bannister. He's not the man for you... I know it, I can feel it in my bones.'

'Oh, Daddy, what are you talking about? You only met him for a second.'

'One's first impression is often the truest one. I tell you, Verity, there's something about him... I saw it in his eyes, in the way he looked at me when we met. A glint of something I didn't like. Oh, he was quick to cover it, but I don't miss things like that.'

'Daddy, it was probably just reaction to the way you were looking at *him*... a nervous reaction.' She dismissed it with a wry smile. 'He would have seen that you were sizing him up, looking for something to dislike or criticise. He's a doctor, he would sense these things.'

Her father gave a snort. 'You just mark my words, pet. Don't say you haven't been warned.'

'Here's our soup,' she said thankfully. She had a feeling it was going to be a long dinner.

Just as Verity was about to leave her apartment the next morning her phone rang. She gritted her teeth as she answered it, vowing that if it were Lorenzo checking up on her movements, she would tell him to get out of her life or she'd move to another state. That should curb his interference in her life.

'Hello?' she said warily.

'Verity! Good morning. Mark here.'

Mark! She felt sweat break out on her palms. 'Good morning,' she said, striving for composure, but quite unable to hide the joy, the relief in her voice. 'Have a good evening last night?'

'Tolerable. I would much rather have spent it with you.'

She swallowed. 'Me too,' she admitted. 'Fathers can be pretty stifling company at times.'

'Mmm...I had the impression he was telling me, "Hands off".'

'Oh, dear, did he make it that obvious? Daddy's hopelessly protective...especially since my aunt died. And since...Donald. Please, don't let it...' She hesitated, on the brink of saying 'stop you seeing me'. Perhaps he hadn't rung for that reason at all, perhaps he'd rung to say...goodbye!

'You're saying you'd defy your father's wishes and agree to see me again?' Mark asked softly.

'He didn't forbid me to see you,' she said, her spirits soaring. He wouldn't dare! 'He just warned me to...be careful of strange men from abroad,' she said lightly.

'Well, that's good.' Understated though it was, she sensed a matching relief in his own voice. 'I have a free lunch-hour today. I thought you might like to meet somewhere. Not too far from the hotel...I'll only have an hour and a half to spare before the afternoon session.'

She didn't hesitate. 'I'd love to,' she said, delight bubbling in her voice. 'What about the Plane Tree at the Hyatt? It's close by, and we could choose from their smorgasbord...'

'Done. Meet you there at twelve?'

'Fine. I'll ring up and book a table. See you there.'

She almost floated from her apartment, floated through the morning, barely noticing what she was doing or where she was going, making sure she left just enough time to slip back to her apartment to freshen up and change before her noon meeting with Mark.

He was already at the Hyatt ahead of her, rising from a lounge chair in the foyer as he spied her.

'You look wonderful,' he said, touching her slender shoulders with the tips of his fingers, his eyes smouldering with a smoky glow as they drank in the sight of her. 'You look as if you've stepped straight from the pages of *Vogue*... or the beauty parlour. Have you?' he teased.

'Far from it,' she said, laughing. 'I've been working all morning. I just popped home to change.' To change from her businesslike skirt and sweater into the long black skirt, cream silk blouse and neat Chanel jacket she was wearing now, and to pull the ribbon from her long plaited hair and brush it loose, leaving the silky tresses in a gleaming black fall down her back.

'Tell me about it over lunch,' Mark said, tucking her arm through his. 'Shall we go in?'

Over lunch he tried gently to draw her out. 'So...what is this work you've been doing all morning?'

She tilted her head at him, noting the sardonic curve of his lips. 'You think I just play at any work I do, don't you?' she said with a rueful smile. But how could she blame him, when she'd been so cautious all along about giving him details?

'You misjudge me...but I confess I am curious. I know you visit sick children in hospital,' he said, 'and I'm aware now that you don't play bridge, or spend your days shopping, or at the hairdresser, or working out at the gym. Let me guess... You rush about raising funds for charity?' he hazarded.

She grimaced. 'I'm not very good at that. But I do work for charitable organisations. I'm more of a background worker, a dogsbody. Nothing high-profile, just doing whatever needs to be done. I work at a centre for disabled children, helping out in the toy library or with the office work when they get snowed under, and I run errands between the various branches. And I also deliver meals to elderly people in their own homes... things like that. The sort of thing anybody can do.'

'But not everybody does,' Mark said. 'It's OK,' he added hastily, holding up his hand. 'I know you don't like making a big thing of it, and I know you don't do it to impress people... I'm *not* impressed,' he assured her with a twitch of his lip. 'I think more people should get in there and help.'

'A lot of people do, only nobody ever hears about them because they don't want any public accolades. They do it because they genuinely care, and because they realise how well off *they* are. And because they have the time—or they *make* the time—to do it.'

He was looking at her in an odd way, she realised. Almost in surprise, as if seeing her in a new light. Why should he feel *surprised*? She felt a twinge of hurt. He couldn't have had a very high opinion of her to begin with! She paused to wonder why. Because until now he'd seen her as a spoilt little rich girl who only played at being an interior designer, who only bothered to work when it suited her? Or perhaps because she was... *who* she was? The daughter of the wealthy and powerful Lorenzo Danza? But he hadn't *known* who she was when they first met...

*Had* he?

'You must sample some of those delectable sweets and cakes on offer,' Mark coaxed, and Verity nodded and followed him back to the smorgasbord table to make their choice.

Over her layered chocolate gâteau and fresh fruit she asked him curiously. 'Have you been divorced long, Mark?' What she really wanted to know was: *Are you still raw from the experience*?

He lifted his broad shoulders and let them fall. 'Years. Eight, going on nine. We were both young—too young—

when we got married. I was a lowly intern then, with many more years of study ahead. Our marriage lasted less than a year.'

So short a time! Was it his work, his long hours spent at the hospital and the extra study load he'd taken on in order to specialise that had come between them? 'Are you still... friends?' she asked tentatively. 'Do you still see each other?'

'Hell, no.' Cynicism hardened his voice. 'She prefers to believe I never existed.'

Verity swallowed a sudden lump in her throat. Did that hardness in his voice mean that he regretted it, that he still... loved her?

'What about you?' she couldn't resist asking. 'Did your break-up hurt you terribly?' *Are you over it*? was what she was really asking.

His mouth twisted. 'Sure you want to hear all this? I don't make a habit of talking about my past mistakes.'

So he considered his marriage a mistake! 'I want to know all about you,' she heard herself confessing, and at once wondered what she was revealing by making such a statement. She asked hurriedly, 'Why was it a mistake?'

He took a mouthful of his fruit flan before answering. 'It never had a hope from the start. We were the wrong two people for each other, and we married for all the wrong reasons. But I hoped we could make it work.'

She gave him a puzzled look. 'You mean—you felt you rushed into it?'

'Not so much that.' Mark shrugged, and set down his spoon. 'Amber and I met when she was selling drugs for a major pharmaceutical company. She was bright company, great fun to be with. We started seeing each other whenever we could. She was a fascinating mixture of child and woman—an adorable child in a woman's body—a heady mix to a serious, hard-working young doctor. But I had no long-term plans in mind when we got...involved. I let her know right from the start that I wasn't ready for any kind of serious commitment, had no plans to settle down, that I intended to specialise, which was going to mean years of hard work and study. She accepted that. She told me she was on the Pill...'

Hearing the icy scorn in his voice, Verity asked softly, 'And she wasn't?'

'No, she wasn't. And yes, you've guessed it. She fell pregnant.'

'And so you told her you'd marry her?'

'Not right away. I told her that was no reason to rush into marriage, but I would support her child if she decided to go ahead and have it. She got hysterical at that, accusing me of wanting her to kill our child.' His mouth hardened. 'I tried to calm her, telling her I'd only meant that it was her own decision and that I'd stand by her no matter what she decided to do. She was inconsolable. She vowed she was going to have the baby, but said she couldn't cope with being a single mother...'

'So you married her,' Verity said in the pause that followed.

'Yes, I married her. I wanted our baby as much as she did...or as much as she made out she did,' Mark amended grimly. 'I wanted to be involved in its upbringing, to be there for the child, all the time, not just as an occasional parent. Fortunately, thanks to my stepfather's generosity, we had no financial worries. I was still able to go on with my studies, as well as finishing my internship at the hospital.'

'And the...baby?' Verity asked hesitantly. Mark had made no previous mention of a son or a daughter.

'There was no baby. It was the oldest trick in the book.' His lip curled. 'And I fell for it.'

'Oh, Mark! What—what did you do? Is that why you divorced her?'

'I didn't divorce her. She divorced *me*, a year or so later. I'd made the commitment, you see, to marry her, and I was prepared to make the best of it. I thought she must really love me to go to such lengths to tie me to her, and I hoped that in time my own feelings for her would grow.'

'But it didn't work out that way?'

He shook his head. 'I was disillusioned only too quickly. Much as she revelled in being the daughter-in-law of a rich Texan oilman and the wife of an up-and-coming young doctor, she wasn't prepared to give anything in return. She complained endlessly about the long hours she spent alone while I was at work or studying, about the way I shamelessly neglected her—much as I tried not to shut her out. She entirely dismissed any need I might have for support or seclusion. I wasn't prepared to give up my lifelong dream to specialise, though I did try to give her more time and attention. But it was never enough. She ended up demanding a divorce. The day I made a generous settlement on her—with my stepfather's help—she got engaged to another man, a guy she'd been secretly seeing for months, and left the state. They're married now. End of story.'

'My... your marriage sounds a real disaster!' Verity's lip quivered. 'Sorry, but there's really no other word for it.'

He gave a lop-sided smile, easing the hard lines of his face. 'No, you're right. I should have known better than to marry her... to marry anyone at that point of my life.'

'I hope it didn't turn you against women for life,' Verity teased, but the question was serious.

His mouth twisted. 'Not against women. Only against matrimony.'

'Well, I feel the same way. Since Donald,' she said. But did she really mean it any more? And why did her spirits suddenly drop?

'Still, who knows what the future holds?' He turned to her, his gaze steadying, focusing on hers, his grey eyes so compelling that she found she couldn't pull her own gaze away, didn't want to pull away.

'There's a cocktail party this evening,' he said, still holding her gaze, but his voice was toneless now, seeming to come from a long way away. 'One of the conference sponsors is putting on a big splash in the Venus Room, and it will be a good opportunity for me to meet a few more people. Why don't you come with me?'

Her eyelids fluttered under his gaze. So he still wanted to go on seeing her. But would it be wise for her to go on seeing *him*? A man who'd sworn off marriage, who was probably only looking for a short-lived affair! She felt confused, unsure of herself for the first time in her life. She could feel herself losing control, falling under his potent spell. She'd be a fool to risk getting any more involved with him.

Misinterpreting her hesitation, Mark drawled, 'I know...cocktail parties can be a dead bore. Trying to juggle drinks and eat at the same time, standing around for hours getting backache, trying to make conversation with people you don't know and often can't stand. But with you there, I reckon I wouldn't notice any of that.' His eyes were beguiling her, paralysing her will.

'Well...' she found her voice. 'I'd hate you to suffer.'

'Is that a yes?'

She nodded. 'Tell me what time and I'll be there.'

# CHAPTER FIVE

'WELL, where have you two been?' boomed Lorenzo Danza, bearing down on Verity and Mark as they stood in the Star Tower's foyer, waiting for the Danza family's private lift.

Verity hid her vexation. Don't you dare start acting the outraged parent, her eyes warned him. Just because Mark is seeing me back to my apartment.

'Mark invited me to a cocktail party,' she said evenly. 'And after that we had a bite of dinner down the street at that spaghetti place.' They had both been glad to escape the cocktail party, leaving as soon as it was decently possible, Mark having already made a few handy contacts. The casual dinner to follow—just the two of them, pleasantly relaxing over a bowl of pasta and a glass of wine—had been wonderful.

'And now you're seeing my daughter home?' Lorenzo asked, shifting his intense gaze to Mark, who met Lorenzo squarely in the eye—which, unlike most men, he did without having to look up—and said smoothly,

'I was...but now that you're here to see her safely to her door, Mr Danza, I'll hand her over to you and take my leave.' As Verity's hand fluttered up in protest, he added easily, 'It's getting late, and I have an early breakfast meeting in the morning before we start our final session.'

His final session...the last day of his conference! *You can't just go*... Her lips opening in panic, Verity transmitted the appeal with her eyes. They had made no arrangement as yet to meet again...she had been waiting

## SHATTERED WEDDING 73

until they were in her apartment. Over dinner they had talked of other things, the people they had met, the work Mark had done back in America, her interest in design and colour, impersonal things. But underneath, every single second, she had been aware of a buzz of excitement, a delicious tension, knowing that Mark would be seeing her home.

'The conference winds up around mid-afternoon,' Mark told them, his cool grey gaze encompassing them both... not, Verity noted in rising panic, focusing on her alone.

She couldn't stand it any longer.

'Have you made any arrangements for the weekend?' she burst out, blithely ignoring her father and the exasperated vibes she could feel emanating from him. 'I was planning to go down to Tarmaroo...'

She had Mark's sole attention now, his eyes colliding with hers.

'Well, I might join you,' he drawled, with an arrogant disregard for Lorenzo's presence. 'Give me a chance to see something of the countryside.'

'Oh, please do!' Verity's face broke into a smile. 'You'll love it down there, Mark. There's so much to see... the Western District farmlands, the Olga Ranges, our Arabian horses, the spectacular coast...'

'My dear...' This time it was her father who intervened, his tone steely-edged. 'I'm sure Dr Bannister can find somewhere more exciting to spend his weekend than a rustic farm buried in country Victoria.'

'On the contrary,' Mark returned silkily, 'a relaxing couple of days in the country, before I start work here, sounds precisely what I need.'

Verity said swiftly, without even glancing at her father, 'Shall we drive down tomorrow afternoon, Mark? Or would you prefer to wait until Saturday morning?'

'Do you normally drive down on Friday evening?' he asked.

'Unless I have a Friday night date in town, yes, which I don't have tomorrow. If we get down there tomorrow night it'll give us two full days at Tarmaroo. I normally drive back Sunday evening, unless it's a long weekend. Or we could drive back on Monday, if you like, to give you longer to look around.' And give me longer in your company, getting to know you better.

'Friday...tomorrow...sounds fine. Any time after, say, four o'clock? No hurry, if you're working.'

'Well, I have promised to spend a few hours at the hospital tomorrow,' Verity said, 'but I'll be back by four. How about I pick you up outside the hotel at four-thirty?'

'You're not driving down with me?' boomed her father, his brow lowering at the turn events were taking.

Verity's heart sank. 'You're coming down too this weekend?'

'There's a polo match at the Bloomfields' place on Saturday. I need the exercise. Do you ride?' he rapped at Mark.

'Sure do. I learnt to ride on my stepfather's ranch in Texas. Spent all my holidays there, riding, mustering, breaking in horses, the whole lot. Even the odd game of polo.'

'Have a game on Saturday,' Lorenzo invited. Show what you're made of, his glinting eyes seemed to be saying.

'Daddy, let's just see...' Verity had visions of her father dragging Mark off to the polo game, away from *her*. 'And I'll take my own car,' she said resolutely. 'You know I prefer to drive myself, so that we can both be independent and go our own ways. I'll be wanting to take Mark for short trips. And you might want to come back before us.' She smiled cajolingly at her father, hidden iron in her smile.

'Well, I'll see you at four-fifteen, Verity,' Mark put in, catching her eye for a brief second. 'Goodnight, Mr Danza.' He thrust out his hand.

Verity held her breath, only releasing it when her father accepted the offered hand. His handshake was perfunctory, but at least, Verity thought in relief, he hadn't openly snubbed Mark.

As she rode up in the lift with her father she berated him. 'You might have been a little more gracious, Daddy. Mark's going to be our house guest. And if you don't treat him——'

'Don't worry,' her father broke in gruffly. 'For your sake I'll be civil to the man. But that doesn't mean——'

This time she was the one who cut in. 'I don't know what you've got against Mark, Daddy. He's one of the finest men I've ever met. You should be happy I've found someone like Mark.'

'*Found*? You talk as if it's serious already.' Lorenzo glowered at her.

'Don't be silly. I've only known him a few days. But if you do anything to spoil it——' she added warningly.

'If he's the fine person you seem to think he is,' muttered her father, 'he has nothing to fear from me.'

'But *you* don't think he is,' she accused as the lift came to a silent stop at her floor.

'I still feel...' He shrugged his great shoulders. 'Call it a sixth sense. It's hard to pin down. I don't trust the man—simple as that. How do we know he's not just after you for your money?'

'He doesn't need our money—ours or anyone else's. He's wealthy in his own right.'

'Maybe he has visions of being even wealthier,' growled her father as the lift doors slid open. 'Doctors tend to have expensive tastes.'

'Mark is probably as wealthy as you are, Daddy—or more!' she shot back, pausing before she stepped out. 'He's recently inherited a huge fortune from his stepfather!'

'Is that what he's told you?' Her father's tone was sceptical as he jammed his finger on the O button to stop the lift door closing.

'I have no reason to doubt him,' Verity retorted coldly. 'He didn't tell me to impress me or anything like that. It just... came up.' She lifted her chin. 'Mark is a very sincere, caring, moral person, Daddy. You'll find out when you get to know him better.'

Lorenzo gave a snort. 'The fellow's clever as well, obviously. What was his stepfather's name?' he bit out. 'If the man was so fabulously wealthy, maybe I've heard of him.'

'I'm not sure Mark mentioned it... no, hang on. Sam somebody.'

'Sam somebody! A great help. How did his stepfather make this immense fortune of his? He had a ranch, I recall your friend saying. Farming?' he sneered.

'Not farming. Oil,' she said with relish. 'I gather there must have been oil on their land in Texas. And Daddy, you're not to grill Mark about it over the weekend. Promise? I'll kill you if you do.'

'Well, *you* promise you'll watch your step. He could be a clever con man for all we know.'

'Oh, Daddy, you're paranoid.' She stepped out of the lift and swung round. 'Just because Mark doesn't lick your boots like other men who chase after me...' An involuntary grin tugged at her lips. 'Who, incidentally, you're equally suspicious of. You'll never approve of any man who looks twice at me!'

Her father grinned back, his finger still pressed to the button. 'I'd approve of young Calder... Alfred Calder's son.'

'Brett Calder?' Verity rolled her eyes. 'I said any man *I* bring home, not the ones—the elite *few*,' she teased, 'that you persist in dangling in front of me. I can't stand any of them!'

'You could do much worse than young Calder. The fellow has everything going for him...looks, perfect manners, impeccable family, and good solid wealth behind him.'

'Wealth?' She pounced on that. 'You expect me to marry for money when you're suspicious of any man who chases after me for *mine*?'

Lorenzo heaved a sigh. 'Of course you don't need a man's money! I'm merely pointing out that the Calders have more than enough of their own, so we can rest easy that Brett won't be chasing after you for yours.'

She laughed scornfully. 'But it's all right if he chases after other women?'

'What do you mean, other women?' Lorenzo frowned at her. 'He's crazy about you. His father told me so.'

'He's crazy about *all* women. He's worse than Donald. Brett Calder has a terrible reputation!'

Lorenzo dismissed the taunt. 'He's just making the most of the fact that he's a highly eligible, popular man about town. Give the fellow a chance, pet...he'll settle down and change his ways. I did...I turned over a new leaf the second I laid eyes on your mother.'

'The *second* you laid eyes on her, yes,' Verity said pointedly, flashing a triumphant smile. 'Brett Calder has laid eyes on me several times, Daddy—I've even been out with him a couple of times—and I see no change in him yet!'

Lorenzo's brow plunged, a sign of defeat. He rallied for one last shot. 'So you're ready to throw yourself away on a man we know nothing about, simply because he's got eyes for nobody but you?'

She threw up her hands in exasperation. 'I'm not ready to throw myself away on anybody...not just yet,' she said through gritted teeth. 'I've only asked Mark for a weekend visit, for heaven's sake. He's just a house guest, like dozens of other house guests we've had. But I *would* like the chance to get to know him better—if that's not too much to ask! Goodnight, Daddy,' she finished firmly, and turned her back on him.

Mark was standing at the kerb with a small suitcase in his hand. As Verity pulled up she called out, 'Hi! Just throw it in the back.' After he'd disposed of it and climbed into the front seat beside her she turned to him and said, 'That can't be all your luggage. Haven't you checked out of the hotel yet?'

'Not yet. I'll hang on to my room until I find a permanent place to live. I still have some things back in the States as well, that I'll send for later.'

'But your room must be costing you——' She broke off, realising it was none of her business if he threw his money around. Obviously he could afford it. 'You intend to look for a house?' she asked instead, as she eased her white Mazda out into the traffic.

'Or an apartment. No hurry—the hotel's fine for now. I want to have a good look around before I buy.'

'Well, if you need wheels just give me a yell.' She concentrated on the traffic ahead as she added carelessly, 'I've taken next week off. I haven't had a break since last year. So I'll have the time...'

'Ma'am, I appreciate that.' But he didn't actually accept her offer, leaving her up in the air, silently kicking herself for telling him now, so soon, about her week off. Damn it, if he thought she was *chasing* him...

They didn't talk for a while, the Friday afternoon traffic already building up, needing all her attention. It was only when they reached the freeway that she ventured to ask Mark,

'Did you feel the paediatrics conference was worthwhile?'

'Mmm, sure.' As he launched into more detail, Verity found herself listening intently, hanging on to his every word, wanting to show him that she was interested in his work, in his thoughts, in his opinions, in *him*.

*In him*? She was aware of a tiny shiver feathering down her spine. This was a new experience for her... Verity Danza, trying to impress a man! She'd never needed to make a particular effort before, had never felt strongly enough—or *weak* enough, she corrected ruefully—about a man to bother. Even Donald, at the height of their courtship, had never made her feel like this, so keen to please, so anxious. Donald had been the one who had done all the impressing, showering her with gifts and flowers, sweeping her off her feet with his generosity and thoughtfulness and his apparent devotion, even sweeping her into his bed once he'd had his ring safely on her finger.

What a sham it had all been! He hadn't cared for her at all. She had actually caught him in bed with another woman, had heard them *laughing* about her, and about another woman he had slept with since their engagement! He had humiliated and disillusioned her. No wonder she found it so hard to trust men now. It was a wonder he hadn't turned her against men for life!

She gripped the steering wheel more tightly as she relived that degrading period of her life. Once the initial shock had passed and the fuss of her broken engagement had died down, she had realised, mercifully, that her feelings for Donald couldn't have gone very deep or she would have felt a lot worse than she did—her heart and her pride could well have been shattered for life! Instead, luckily, she had come through with her heart bruised but relatively intact. Bitter as she had been, she had found herself, in the end, feeling almost grateful to Donald, relieved that he had shown his true colours well before they had reached the altar—if not before she had allowed him certain liberties she had previously allowed no other man!

'What the——?' She swerved to avoid another car flashing across her path at an intersection. She hadn't even seen it coming!

'Sorry!' she gasped, silently thanking her lucky stars that she had missed the car. If they had collided, she would have been the one at fault. Concentrate, you fool, she railed at herself. Keep your mind on the road!

She felt Mark's hand on hers, heard him ask softly, 'You OK?' and was aware of a tingling warmth flowing through her. Donald would have berated her. He wouldn't have tried to comfort her, or shown concern for her.

'I'm just fine,' she said, and thought, I'm falling for this guy. It's sheer madness, I know, but I *am*. Dear Lord, please, *please* let him be the man I think he is... and not another Donald!

She slid a furtive glance sideways, hugging to herself the thought that she would have him to herself for at least the next three days.

A lot could happen in three days.

'Beautiful countryside,' Mark commented as they drove through the open rolling pasture typical of western Victoria's prime pastoral country, the rich green undulating hills glowing emerald in the orange rays of the setting sun.

'It always looks its best in the spring,' she returned, pleased that he too saw it as beautiful. 'Everything is still green and lush after the winter rains. But even at the height of summer, it's still lovely down here.' It was a high-rainfall area, where the sandy loam drained easily in a wet winter, and the heavier clay slopes, many of which faced away from the sun, provided excellent grazing during the summer.

'I love it down here,' she added impulsively, feeling her usual surge of warmth and pride as they passed through the gates of her family's property, the cares of the past week slipping from her shoulders as the car swept along the graded road between the paddocks.

And I hope you'll love it here too, she thought, willing the man beside her to see Tarmaroo with her eyes, to feel the same sense of peace and homecoming as she did. Mark no longer had a home of his own. He needed a place he could call home, or could think of as his home, until he found somewhere of his very own. It would be wonderful if he could come to look on Tarmaroo in the same way she did... as a haven to come back to.

A property of several thousand hectares, Tarmaroo lay at the edge of the Otways, a few kilometres south of the town of Colac. The original owners of the property had cleared dense bush from the land, leaving some magnificent trees—peppermint and swamp gums, messmate and manna gums—to act as shade and shelter in the cleared paddocks. Belts of timber a chain wide stood undisturbed between the paddocks, and untouched trees had been left around the springs of clear sweet water which abounded.

'What kind of cattle do you run?' asked Mark, nodding in the direction of a herd of cattle grazing in the lush paddocks.

'Murray Grey beef cattle. Our manager, Tom O'Reilly, who lives in a cottage on the property with his wife Dee— who incidentally cooks and cleans for us—does a great job. Now that my aunt has... gone, the horse stud is being looked after by a marvellous girl—Georgia Stone, an ex-pupil of my aunt's. Georgia already seems like one of the family. She lives here as well, in our house. She's only my age, but she's very competent. She has her hands full with the stud, and with her teaching and shows.'

'Arabian horses,' Mark recalled.

'That's right. If you look over there,' Verity nodded in the direction of a rustic-fenced paddock, 'you'll see some of our mares with their foals. They run out all year round. We don't believe in keeping them under wraps. Even our stallions have their own paddocks, out where they can see the mares. It's never seemed to bother them.'

'They look fine animals.'

'Aren't they beautiful? They're all quality Arabians. My aunt was devoted to them, as Georgia is. They've always done extremely well in the show ring. But we look on them first and foremost as family friends.'

Mark turned in his seat, and she felt his eyes on her as she drove on. But when he spoke it was to ask, 'How many horses would you have here?'

'I'd say around forty pure Arabians. We also bring in outside mares. We have three stallions, all champions, with many wins to their credit.'

An avenue of huge poplars brought them to elaborate iron gates in a walled garden. Passing through, they followed a long drive flanked by rhododendrons and azaleas, behind which they could see thick pine trees and a graceful gazebo in an expanse of rich green lawn, until they reached the house, approaching it from the side, the drive swelling into a broad gravel apron in front of the main door.

'Welcome to Tarmaroo,' Verity said, pulling up by the front steps.

'Most obliged to you, ma'am. I can see why you love coming home at weekends,' Mark said, the corner of his lip tilting. 'Simple, homely country farm, huh?'

'It *is* homely. You'll find it very comfortable,' she assured him, anxiously following his gaze as he took in the long low-spreading lines of the old Victorian house with its broken roofline of corrugated iron and its charming bay windows and attractive white shutters. Built of heavy grey bluestone, the walls were softened by a separately roofed cast-iron veranda heavy in wistaria. Separate balancing pavilions were set back behind the main block. Extra pavilions, Verity told Mark, had been added over the years, including a bedroom wing and a billiard-room and study, while various other alterations had been carried out over time.

'The house was built in 1885,' she added. 'Late Victorian, with some neo-Georgian touches. The pavilion to the left is an Edwardian addition.' She threw open her door and Mark did likewise, pulling out his suitcase as he stepped out.

'Well, shall we go in?' she said, knowing that Georgia would be expecting them to join her for a drink before dinner, and she was sure Mark would want to freshen up and change first. She certainly did. She was still wearing the crumpled skirt and blouse she had been wearing all day.

She led him up the wide front steps, across the tiled veranda to the heavily panelled front door. As she reached for the shiny brass knocker she had a crazy insane image of Mark carrying her across the threshold one day... maybe not this threshold, but the threshold of their very own home, wherever it might be. Was she mad to be thinking this way, having such dreams? And so soon? Heavens, Mark hadn't even kissed her yet. He'd barely even touched her! Not that he'd had much time, much opportunity...

But if he had really wanted to...

She glanced up at him in sudden doubt. Other men, by now, would have at least tried to kiss her, or found some other way to show their interest in her. Mark seemed almost to be... holding back, keeping an invisible wall between them. Was it the memory of his wife's betrayal that was inhibiting him? Or was it simply that he didn't want to get involved with anyone at this point of his life, uncertain and unsettled as his future was? Or had he made up his mind not to get emotionally entangled with Verity Danza in particular, and that was the reason he was keeping her at arm's length?

She was being silly, she knew. Expecting too much, too soon. They'd only known each other a few days! And he'd agreed to spend the weekend with her, hadn't he? Give him time, Verity, you fool, she told herself. The man's been burnt once already by a woman, just as you've been burnt yourself. It takes time to learn to trust again—you should know.

He was facing away from her, looking out over the charming garden in front of the house. It was worth a second look, she couldn't deny, laid out as it was in symmetrical looped paths edged with box hedgings, with a glimpse of a rusticated summerhouse among the trees. His expression was closed, even a trifle remote. What was he thinking? she wondered, her breath tightening in her throat. If only she knew!

'Verity!' The front door swung open and Georgia was there, smiling a welcome, her sleek blonde hair pulled back with a red ribbon, her tiny waist accentuated by her figure-hugging moleskins and tucked-in shirt. She had never looked more attractive, Verity thought, noting with a twinge the openly curious, provocative look Georgia was giving Mark. Or was she just imagining that it was provocative? She'd never experienced jealousy before in her life. Was this what it felt like? She dismissed the idea with scorn.

'Georgia, it's great to be home,' she said with genuine warmth—she *liked* Georgia—and turning, let her hand flutter towards Mark. 'Georgia, this is Dr Mark Bannister, from America. He'll be staying with us for

# SHATTERED WEDDING

the weekend. I'm sure he's looking forward to some fresh country air, after being buried in a medical conference all week.' She felt a tiny shock jolt through her as Mark touched the hand she was holding out to him—only to feel it slide away an instant later as he extended the same hand to Georgia.

After they had exchanged a few pleasantries—was Georgia always as vivacious as this? Verity wondered, aware of another brief pang—she said, 'Mark, let me show you to your room,' and turning to Georgia asked, 'You'll meet us for pre-dinner drinks at our usual time?' half hoping Georgia would have something else in mind for the evening.

'Fine,' Georgia said with a smile, a smile that to Verity seemed brighter than usual, and directed solely at Mark.

'Nice girl,' Mark remarked as she led him through the beautifully restored living-room on their way to the bedroom wing. The long room always looked warmly inviting with its scattered rugs and comfortable rust-coloured couches and deep green patterned armchairs. A welcoming fire had been lit already in the open stone fireplace.

'Very nice,' Verity agreed, adding pointedly, 'I'm hoping that one day she and my brother Johnny might—well, you know.' She waved an expressive hand, her sapphire eyes twinkling. 'They were just starting to notice each other when Daddy sent my brother off to America.'

'Your father would approve of the match?' Mark asked. Was he disappointed? Verity pondered uneasily.

She snapped her mind back to Mark's question. 'Oh, yes, I would think so. My aunt certainly would have been all for it,' she said, a wistful note creeping into her voice.

He glanced down at her. 'You miss your aunt, don't you?'

She nodded. 'She was like a mother to me. She *was* my mother,' she amended. 'I never knew any other.'

'And in all these years your father has never remarried.' Mark's tone was bemused. 'I guess he's made his business his overriding obsession...taking the place of a wife?'

Verity pursed her lips. 'Daddy might be a workaholic, but I wouldn't call it an obsession. His family have always come first. And he hasn't exactly spurned women,' she added with a smile. Reminded of her father, she said, half to herself, 'I wonder if Daddy's going to be here for dinner?'

'You sound a little apprehensive about it.' Mark gave her a quizzical look. 'I hope it's not on my behalf?'

'Well, Daddy can be a trifle...overbearing at times,' she admitted with a sigh. 'Especially when I bring a friend home who happens to be male. Please don't let it——' She paused, hesitant to finish what she had started to say. *Scare you away*, she had almost said. Whether Mark was interested in her or not, he didn't need her to defend him. Mark was a man who could more than stand up to her father. 'His bark is worse than his bite, really it is,' she finished with a rallying smile.

He smiled back, a smile tinged with irony. 'Look, I'm aware your father's not over-happy having an unknown American hanging around his daughter. I'd feel the same, I reckon, if I were in his place, if I had a beautiful daughter who was going to come into a share of the family fortune.'

'He does get a bit paranoid,' she agreed, thankful that Mark understood, and feeling a tiny thrill that he thought her beautiful.

'Guess you can't blame him.' He looked down at her. 'He's coming home to relax and unwind for a couple of days. How can a guy relax and talk openly with his family, knowing there's a stranger in the house, knowing he'll have to watch every word he utters? A careless word, a name dropped...well, I could be a danger to your father, couldn't I, for all he knows?'

Verity gave him a reassuring smile as she ushered him into the green room, the bedroom Dee had prepared for him. 'Please, Mark, there's no need to concern yourself...my father has no secrets, nothing to hide. I doubt if he'd even worry if you were a business rival. My father has many friends in the property business— in all areas he's involved in. If he likes and respects someone, he doesn't let petty rivalry come between them. He's remarkably open and down-to-earth. And honest. I think that's why he's so highly respected in the business world. People trust my father. He's known for his sincerity and integrity.'

Mark made no comment to that, but she knew he was absorbing it and, she hoped, was feeling reassured by it.

'Very comfortable,' he said, looking around. 'Grand, but comfortable.' He was looking at the big four-poster bed as he spoke, and she felt herself flushing. Averting her face quickly, she pulled open another door.

'*En-suite* bathroom,' she told him. 'You'll find fresh towels and various toiletries in there. Anything else you need, just call out. Think you can find your way back to the lounge?' she asked, and when he nodded, his lips curving into that crooked, captivating smile of his that could turn her limbs to water, she said quickly, 'I'll meet you there in half an hour,' and turned tail and fled.

## CHAPTER SIX

'DADDY not here yet?' Verity asked Georgia as they settled in front of the open fire with their cool drinks. Mark was already looking comfortably at home in one of the big armchairs, having changed into casual trousers and a sports shirt with a loosely tied cravat at his throat. He was fresh from a shower, his hair still damp, combed to one side, with a few spiky hairs falling across his brow. He looked so at ease, so ruggedly attractive, so heart-rendingly *male* that she could barely look at him, barely believe that she had him to herself—well, almost to herself—for a whole weekend.

He hadn't lingered with Georgia when he first came into the room, though Georgia's cool blonde beauty had never been more alluring, her sleek hair softly framing her face and her vibrant blue sweater enhancing its golden highlights. Instead, he had moved straight over to *her*, his smoky eyes skimming over her fresh cream blouse and fringed leather shirt before dwelling for a heart-stopping moment on her face, the grey depths burning silver-bright under her gaze.

'You look great, Verity,' he'd said to her, and her heart had swelled at the compliment, even though she'd heard the trite phrase a thousand times before without feeling the slightest flutter. Her exhilaration added a violet brilliance to her eyes and a rosy lustre to her cheeks, making her, if she only knew it, even more strikingly beautiful.

'Your father rang to say he's having dinner in town,' Georgia told her. 'He'll be coming down later tonight.'

Verity's spirits lifted further. Her father's presence at dinner could have put a dampener on the evening.

'Tom's joining us for dinner,' Georgia added, and Verity explained to Mark,

'Our manager Tom O'Reilly and his wife Dee, our housekeeper, often have dinner here with us, to save Dee having to cook another meal when she goes home. Ah, speak of the devil!'

A small nuggety man strolled in, his thin brown face deeply lined from his years spent out in the sun. Tom had been with the family for years, Verity told Mark in an undertone. He'd married Dee, widowed like himself, not long after Dee had come to Tarmaroo to replace their long-time housekeeper, who had suffered a stroke.

Verity made the introductions, calling Dee in from the kitchen to join them for a drink. Dee, plump and good-natured, with an infectious deep-bellied laugh, accepted, popping in and out at intervals to check on the dinner. It was a family atmosphere, easy and relaxed, with the conversation lively at times, ranging from farm matters and horse shows to the weather, with a dash of politics thrown in. Verity sensed that Mark was quietly enjoying himself...sensed a tinge of surprise in him too, at the warmth and informality he was finding in the Danza home.

Dinner in the intimate red-carpeted dining-room, with its soft antique lamps and red flock wallpaper, with a bowl of fresh flowers in the centre of the highly polished mahogany table, was an equally lively affair. Dee had prepared a superb meal of tasty onion soup and herbed roast lamb with home-grown vegetables, with smooth brown gravy and fresh mint sauce, topping it off with her special baked apple pie, served with thick clotted cream.

'I haven't had a good home-cooked meal like this for years,' Mark said approvingly, and Dee glowed under his praise.

They had their coffee in front of the lounge-room fire, then Dee slipped away to clean up the kitchen, refusing all offers of help. When she had finished, she and Tom excused themselves and went home to their own cottage, and shortly after that Georgia yawned and rose to take her leave too.

'I have to be up early—it's a specially busy time for me, with the royal show coming up soon,' she told Mark with a smile. Mark's mouth stretched into an answering smile as he rose from his chair to bid her goodnight, and Verity felt her stomach knotting.

Did those shared smiles mean anything? she brooded, and was immediately disgusted with herself. She'd always despised jealous females. For heaven's sake, they'd only *smiled* at each other!

She gave Georgia a specially bright smile of her own and snuggled deeper into her chair. At least she had Mark to herself now... for a short while, at least. Her father, as she was only too aware, could walk in at any moment.

She opened her mouth to speak just as Mark turned his back on her to kneel down and poke at the fire.

She gulped back the words she had been about to utter. Was he deliberately turning away from her, deliberately putting distance between them? Uncertainty flared inside her. It was an odd feeling, a bewildering feeling, not knowing where she stood with a man. Any other man, left alone with her, would have been all over her within seconds!

But if he wasn't interested in her, then why had he come? It wasn't as if she had pressed him to come, making it difficult for him to refuse... he'd practically invited himself!

Stifling a sigh, she let her gaze rove over his bent head, down over the broad spread of his shoulders, her eyes feasting on the ripple of his muscles as he stoked the fire. She tensed as he replaced the poker with a sharp clang of metal on metal, and settled back in his chair. 'That should help a bit,' he said easily. 'Hardly worth putting on another log at this hour.'

'No, I guess not.' Was that another brush-off? Or was she being ultra-sensitive, imagining things again? Verity gave herself a tiny shake. She was expecting too much too quickly... and over-reacting as a result. She'd only imagined that he had turned away from her, only imagined Georgia was trying to beguile him, only imagined that he'd responded. What was *wrong* with her?

Whatever might have happened next was thwarted by her father's arrival, his big hulk suddenly filling the doorway as he threw open the door in his usual bombastic fashion, the fire in the grate crackling to renewed life in the sudden draught that swept through the room with him.

'Meant to be home sooner,' he boomed, his dark gaze raking over the two of them as he marched across the room, the fire in his eyes losing some heat as he noted the respectable distance between them and the way Mark was already rising to his feet, his hand outstretched. 'Where's Georgia?' Lorenzo growled, looking at Verity as he shook Mark's hand.

'She's just gone to bed,' Verity said with a defiant lift of her chin, her eyes warning him not to start throwing his weight around.

Lorenzo's brow lowered a fraction at her answer, as if he suspected that Mark might have made a suggestion along similar lines—to his daughter. 'Do you play snooker, Doctor?' His eyes snapped round to trap Mark's.

Mark spread his hands. 'I haven't played since my university days so I'd be a bit rusty.' He lifted a mocking eyebrow as he added impassively, 'And the name's Mark.'

Verity expected her father to growl 'Lorenzo' in return, as he would have with almost anyone else, but he didn't. An ominous sign, she thought, sighing. He was determined not to be easily won over.

'Let's find out just how rusty you are,' he rapped at Mark. 'Verity, my dear, if you want to get your beauty sleep...'

'I don't,' she said through gritted teeth. 'I'll come and watch.'

'As you wish.' Her father turned on his heel. 'I'll get out of this suit and be right with you.'

'Want some coffee?' Verity called after him.

'No, thanks. You might pour us both a port, though... unless you'd rather have a cognac, Doctor?'

'A port will be fine, thanks... Mr Danza.' There was a tinge of irony in Mark's voice. 'Doctor' and 'Mr Danza' it was going to continue, for now.

'He's just trying you out, seeing what you're made of,' Verity sighed as her father vanished from sight. 'He can be such a bear!' She gave Mark a quick smile. 'I hope you beat him.'

'That might not be diplomatic.' Mark smiled back, but it was a smile curiously lacking in humour. 'Even if I were capable. I haven't played in years.'

'If you can beat him, go for it,' Verity urged. 'Daddy's not a poor loser, thank heaven. He'll respect you more if you don't kowtow to him and let him win. If he beats *you*—well, he'll respect you just as much if you put up a good fight.'

'Oh, I intend to do that...' Mark's tone had changed imperceptibly. There was a cold, indefinable expression in his eyes, a hint of iron in his jaw, and the smile on his lips had changed too, hardened.

Verity saw it and shivered. It's the thought of the challenge ahead, she thought. To both men, obviously, the encounter was going to be more a power play than a mere game. Two strong men, pitting their wills—and their skills—against each other.

'I'll be there,' she assured him, 'to cheer you on.'

'Then let battle commence,' said Mark, brushing the air with his hand. Before letting it drop he reached out and let his fingertips trail, ever so lightly, across her cheek. As she tried not to react openly to his touch, inwardly she was thrilling at it, eagerly absorbing it, drinking it in as if it were water being offered someone dying of thirst.

And then it was gone.

Lorenzo's swagger lasted only as long as their initial foray at the table. To Verity's delight, Mark proved a formidable opponent, and the older man needed all his wits and skill to match his younger, sharper opponent.

'Rusty, eh?' Lorenzo muttered with grudging respect as Mark holed yet another ball.

'It must be like riding a bicycle,' Mark excused his prowess with an apologetic shrug. 'Amazing how it all comes back,' he said as he holed the black, the last ball on the table. 'Want another game, Mr Danza?' he asked, straightening. 'Or would you like to take on your daughter this time?'

Lorenzo glanced at his watch. 'My daughter should be in bed,' he said gruffly, 'and so should I.' He raised a brow at Mark, who took the hint and said solemnly,

'Well, then, I reckon I'll turn in myself. Maybe tomorrow night, Mr Danza, you might like to get your revenge.'

'Since you've offered me the chance, why not?' Lorenzo's black eyes glinted as he accepted the challenge. 'The chance for revenge is always sweet.'

'Revenge can be sweet, so they say,' Mark agreed. His lips were smiling, Verity noted, but his eyes, oddly, were not. It struck her then just how much he must have wanted to win tonight, or at least to put up a good fight against her father. He looked—spoke—as if it had meant more to him than just a game. She gave him a bright, understanding smile. Her father, she knew, could have that effect on people. He often brought out the fight in them.

'We usually have breakfast around nine o'clock,' she told Mark as they left the room together, 'but please, feel free to get up at any time. Georgia's always up early, seeing to her horses and feeding the chickens and cats and dogs, and I usually give her a hand before breakfast.'

'Well, if you intend to be up early,' Mark drawled, 'I may join you. If you'll both excuse me...' his smile, tipping crookedly at the corners, took in them both, not lingering too long on Verity '...I'll leave you, with thanks for a pleasant night—and a good game. Goodnight, Verity. Goodnight, sir.'

Lorenzo lifted a hand in a grudging salute as Mark left the room. As Verity moved to follow him her father rapped, 'Just a minute.'

She turned, balling her small hands into fists, frustration quivering through her as she watched Mark's back disappear. 'Yes, Daddy?' This is a conspiracy, she thought, heaving a sigh. At this rate, I'll never even get a goodnight kiss... let alone anything more!

'You're bringing our guest to the polo game tomorrow?' Lorenzo asked her, his tone less aggressive now, even cajoling. He knew full well that she was aware of what he was up to!

'If I have anything to do with it—no!' she said unequivocally, sapphire sparks livening her eyes. 'If Mark's agreeable, I intend taking him for a drive through the Otway Ranges to the coast. Just the two of us!'

'Well, you take care,' Lorenzo muttered, realising he'd pushed her too far. If he'd used a more diplomatic approach, she just might have brought her doctor friend to the polo match, where he could have shown that arrogant American upstart a thing or two on the polo field. Now, through his crass stupidity, he'd lost his chance. Daughters! They turned a man into a damned fool at times!

Verity woke early, after a restless night. She refreshed herself under a hot shower, pulled on jeans and a sweater, and, tying her long mass of hair in a loose ponytail, slipped from her room—almost colliding with Mark in the passage.

'I thought I heard you moving around,' he said, fingering his unshaven jaw with a wry smile. 'I know you said you rise early down here, but I wasn't expecting you to be up with the birds.'

She looked up at him, for a second finding herself completely tongue-tied. Seeing Mark here in her home at this early hour of the morning, looking so husky and unkempt, so virile in his jeans and T-shirt, his hair still ruffled from his night's sleep and his face looking tougher, more ruggedly male than ever with its overnight growth, had thrown her a bit. 'I'm sorry,' she managed finally. 'Did I wake you?'

His smile stretched wider. 'Hell, no! I was just surprised, that's all, to find you so fresh and perky so early in the morning.'

She moistened her lips with a flick of her tongue. Did he still see her as an idle, pampered rich man's kid? She dragged her eyes away from his.

'When you work with horses you get used to it. Coming?' she said lightly, and strode away from him, seizing the chance, when her back was safely turned, to regain her composure with a deep indrawn breath. Whatever he thought of her, or *felt* for her, if anything, Dr Mark Bannister was the most intriguing, frustrating, totally fascinating man she had ever met!

The morning chill hit them as they walked out of the back door. A fine mist hung over the property, though it promised to be a fine day later. There was a large service area behind the house, with stables and sheds and small fenced paddocks, all well maintained, and set to advantage among the lovely old trees—Norfolk pines and native gums and big old English oaks and elms. Georgia, wrapped up in a parka, was already there, attending to a magnificent chestnut Arabian mare.

'Mark, meet Queenie.' Verity waved her hand. 'Officially Tarmaroo Queen.'

'She's competing in the royal show again this year,' Georgia told Mark, her suntanned hand stroking the mare's velvety nose. 'Incredibly statuesque, isn't she? A brilliant show mare. She sails into the arena with the presence and dignity of the *Queen Elizabeth*. Last year she won supreme champion, over all the other horses, stallions included.'

'Georgia's won hundreds of ribbons herself,' Verity put in, pushing any jealousy firmly aside, deciding it was too souring an emotion. Dropping her voice, she added, 'She rides like an angel. And always looks immaculate when she goes off to a show... and so do her horses.' Damn it, she *liked* Georgia—she couldn't help it. She was almost like a sister.

'I can imagine.' Mark's gaze flicked over Georgia as if he were picturing her in a black riding hat, frilly shirt and trim trousers. 'And what about you?' he asked, looking at Verity.

'Me?' She gulped as she met his eye, his attention now for her alone. 'Oh, I've ridden in a few shows, but I'd rather ride just for fun. And I love helping around the stud. Like to go over and see Gem now? Tarmaroo Gem, to be exact. He's one of our stallions.'

She led Mark to a holding paddock where a big mottled grey horse with pointed ears and large eyes stood close to the fence, his black mane lifting as he tossed his head at their approach.

'We imported him from Egypt twelve years ago,' Verity told Mark. 'He's been our most valuable sire. He's also a good working horse, the best working cattle horse Tom says he's ever ridden.'

'You really love it here, don't you?' Mark commented, glancing down at her, his eyebrow lifting.

Unsure if he was being critical of her easy lifestyle, she let her gaze flutter away from his. Her hand was trembling as she reached out to stroke Gem's silky neck. Because in the split second before she had plucked her gaze away from Mark's she had glimpsed something in the grey depths that had shaken her—not condemnation, not derision, but a tiny flame, a flash of awareness, a sizzle of white heat that had seared across the narrow space between them.

She was tempted to glance back at him, but the thought that she might have imagined it, or worse, might have mistaken a burning contempt for a flame of a softer kind, stopped her. Why risk disappointment? Best to keep her spirits buoyant, to believe what she dearly wanted to believe!

'Yes, I do love it here,' she admitted quietly, her eyes on Gem. 'It's been great for Johnny and me... it's given us a safe, happy, stable environment. Tarmaroo's always been home to us, a haven, an escape... an escape from boarding-school and college and the pressures of life in the city. Didn't you find the same thing with your ranch in Texas?'

'Sure. It's good you feel the same way.'

She dared to look at him then, but he'd turned away, his eye caught by a powerful red stallion galloping across an adjacent paddock, mane and tail flying.

'That's Tarmaroo Sultan,' she said. 'Magnificent, isn't he? All presence and pizazz—a real dynamo.'

'And by the look of him, supremely confident of his own importance,' Mark commented.

The horse trotted up to the fence as they approached, moving with big floating paces, arching his neck, swishing his tail, supremely elegant, with a proud arrogance in every line of his magnificent body.

'He's been a great show horse,' Verity told Mark. 'He moves like a dream—full of arrogance and charisma. He seems to cover incredible distances without even touching the ground.'

She led Mark away to see the other stallion, Tarmaroo King.

'King's great to ride,' she told him. 'He's a breeding stallion, but he's also very much our family horse. He's a true gentleman—proud and exuberant, but also sensible. Like to take him for a ride later?'

'I thought you might have offered me Sultan.' There was a thread of humour in Mark's voice. 'To see what I'm made of.'

'Reckon you can handle him?' Verity challenged, looking up at him provocatively—only to be jolted at the sight of the same tiny flame she had glimpsed earlier, kindling deep in the grey depths. This time she didn't glance away, letting her gaze cling to his, but when she saw the flame die, coldly extinguished, she wished that she had, her heart sinking in dismay at the implication of that abrupt withdrawal. He does feel something, she thought, but he doesn't *want* to, won't let himself give in to it. *Why*? Because he still didn't trust women, after what his wife did to him all those years ago? Or had there been another even deeper hurt since?

'I'm sure your father would be delighted if Sultan threw me on my head.' Mark's voice was heavy with irony. 'Are you sure he didn't suggest Sultan himself?'

'Oh, Mark, how can you think such a thing of my father!' She laughed, and shook her head. 'He doesn't have a vindictive bone in his body!'

'No? There are some who think otherwise.' Mark's tone was bantering, but his eyes were narrowed, mere slits against the misty sun. 'From what I've heard.'

'Oh? *What* have you heard?' she demanded, frowning. She wouldn't have thought that Mark was the type to listen to empty, malicious gossip—and that was all it could be. Surely he knew that any man of wealth and power, no matter how high-principled and honest, was an easy target for gossip and jealous innuendo.

Mark shrugged. 'You pick up talk around hotels. You catch the name Danza...pick up a passing comment. "Danza's ruthless in his business dealings"..."Danza doesn't suffer rivals gladly"...'

Verity pursed her lips, her brow furrowing. Rivals? Had Mark overheard something about her father's casino bid? About his rivalry with Jack Hammond over securing the bid? Was that what he was referring to?

For a moment the air hung between them, neither of them moving or speaking, tension building in the awkward silence.

Finally she broke it, muttering, 'I'm surprised you listen to idle gossip.' And disappointed too, her pained eyes told him. Her father might have privately criticised Hammond for his unwise business practices and his insatiable greed for more and more property, and even gloated over the company's shaky finances, but he'd never spoken out publicly or taken any action to hurt Hammond, other than trying to secure the casino bid for himself. What was ruthless or wrong about that? she wondered.

'My father's done nothing to be ashamed of!' she burst out.

Mark caught her arm. 'Verity, forgive me. Look, believe me, I admire the way you stand up for your father, and believe in him. Your father's a lucky man to have a loyal, loving daughter like you.'

His touch electrified her; her skin seared under the grip of his fingers. She felt her body weakening, her limbs turning to water, but she wasn't ready to forgive him just yet.

'I believe in him because he's worth believing in,' she said, her voice throbbing with sincerity. 'Mark, please don't listen to what a few jealous, misguided people might say or think. Get to know my father for yourself. You'll see that he's everything I've said he is. Anyone who knows him or works with him—and I'm including his rivals in the property business—would say the same.'

Mark had no chance to comment, even if he'd intended to; his head jerked round as a shout came from the yard. 'I think Georgia's calling us.'

Verity glanced at her watch. 'Nine o'clock already!' She gave Georgia a wave. 'Time for breakfast.'

'First say you've forgiven me.' His hand was still on her arm. Not tightly, but she couldn't have moved, couldn't have pulled away if she'd tried!

'Nothing to forgive,' she said lightly, smiling to show she meant it. I'd forgive you anything, she thought recklessly, as their eyes met for a brief, tremulous second. Then he flicked his gaze away and dropped his hand.

'We'd better get going.'

\* \* \*

'No sign of Daddy yet?' Verity asked as they strolled into the glassed-in conservatory, a recent addition to the house, where they usually had breakfast. Dee had spread out an array of cereals and fresh fruits and croissants to choose from, along with a jug of freshly-squeezed orange juice, and was now waiting to take orders from anyone who wanted a cooked breakfast.

'He's in the den,' said Dee. 'He had a phone call, and then I heard the television go on. Will you go and ask him what he wants, love, and if he wants me to start cooking?'

Verity caught Mark's eye. 'Help yourself to some orange juice. I won't be a minute.'

She found her father perched in front of the TV set watching a business programme. He gave her a quick self-satisfied smile and waved her away.

'Jack Hammond's about to make an announcement.' Lorenzo could barely hide his jubilation. 'He's pulling out of the casino bid—he must be. Unless it's even worse, and his company has collapsed. Poor coot, I almost feel sorry for him.'

'Then stop looking as if you've just licked the cream bowl,' Verity teased. 'Want a cooked breakfast?'

'Sh!' He leaned forward. 'No, nothing.'

She took the hint and left him. Mark glanced round as she rejoined him in the conservatory. 'Your father's not joining us for breakfast?'

'No. He's watching a business programme on television. I've already told Dee he doesn't want anything. I hear she's persuaded you, on the other hand, to have sausages, bacon and eggs?' Verity tilted her head at him as she poured herself a glass of orange juice. 'You follow the school that believes in a hearty breakfast?'

'It's the country air. It's given me a hearty appetite.' He pulled out a chair for her and they both sat down at the white cast-iron table. 'So it's off to the polo game today?' he asked.

She drew in a quick breath. 'Well, I was thinking of taking you for a drive through the Otways to Port Campbell...'

'You don't want to go to the polo game?' Mark looked surprised.

She was about to shake her head and respond with some lighthearted quip, but the suspicion that he might want to play polo held her back. 'Do you want to?' she asked, burying a twinge of disappointment that he hadn't leapt at the chance to be alone with her.

'Well, I haven't played in ages. Too many years spent buried in textbooks,' he said, his mouth tilting in a smile.

How could she refuse him anything when he smiled at her like that? She swallowed, and nodded.

'We can always go for a drive tomorrow,' she said, summoning a smile of her own. 'Maybe when we get back from the game, if it's not too late, we could go for a ride then.'

'Sounds great.' He turned his head as Dee sailed in with his hot breakfast. 'Mmm...a breakfast fit for a king.'

Dee giggled.

Verity stifled a sigh as she bent her glossy dark head over her bowl of muesli. So now they were committed to spending the day with her father. Mark had thrown away the chance of a whole day alone with her in favour of a country polo match and another lively duel with her father! The thought drew a faint frown. Anyone would think that Mark was more interested in her father than in her!

*Was* he? A niggling doubt riffled through her. Mark had asked quite a few questions about her father, she recalled, since he had found out who she was... or since she had *revealed* who she was. Could he already have known? She'd sometimes wondered. Mistaking her for the florist could have been a cunning ploy to pull the wool over her eyes.

No! She refused to believe that Mark could have had some shady, underlying motive for seeking her company. They had met purely by chance!

If she hadn't known him to be a highly respected doctor, only recently arrived from America, she might have had reason to doubt, to wonder what his motivation might be, or if he could have been sent by someone, by another company perhaps, or even by the taxation department, to ask questions and spy on the family. Verity stifled a giggle at the thought that Mark might be an income-tax spy. He'd find no joy if he were. Her father was no tax cheat.

'May I share the joke?'

She looked up and found Mark's eyes on her, speculation in the cool grey.

She smiled openly then. 'Just thinking of Daddy,' she said evasively. 'He should enjoy his game today—he's in a good mood. His bid for the Melbourne casino is looking brighter than ever,' she added. Why not be open with Mark? It was only natural for him to be curious, to want to know more about them. Men of great wealth and power, sadly, often *were* corrupt, as most people, Mark included, must be aware. Mark simply needed reassurance that her father wasn't like that—that he was a man of honesty and integrity, like himself.

Anyway, it was the polo game Mark was interested in today, not so much her father. He hadn't had a game for years, he'd said. She was overreacting again, her ego dented at being pushed into second place.

'Your father's confident of winning the Melbourne casino bid?' Mark's brow shot up.

Verity nodded. 'And he does want it so badly.' She frowned suddenly. 'I thought he'd have made an appearance by now.' She set down her spoon and pushed back her chair. 'Would you excuse me, Mark? I'll take him some coffee. If he doesn't get a move on, he'll be late for the polo game.'

'Sure, go ahead.'

She rose, poured a cup of coffee and headed for the den, the jangle of the TV set muffling her footsteps as she walked in.

'Daddy!' she cried, spilling coffee into the saucer in her haste to reach his side. He sat rigid in his chair, his fists clenched, his eyes frozen in a look of shocked outrage. 'Daddy, what is it? What's wrong?' She put the coffee down with a clatter and dropped on to the arm of his chair, sliding her arm round his shoulders.

Startled, he looked up, the stunned look in his eyes flaring into a blazing white fury.

'That cunning, conniving devil!' he roared. 'I might have known it was too good to be true.'

'Daddy! You mean——'

'I mean Hammond's found a way out, drat the man. He's formed a consortium with some overseas company—they've hushed up who it is—and his casino bid is going ahead, with this foreign company pouring in the finance. According to Hammond, they have enough money at their disposal to build the greatest casino in the world—and they intend offering the Government better terms than anyone else would be crazy enough to offer. Nobody else can hope to compete. I've had it!'

'Daddy, you don't *know* yet... You've only heard Hammond's side, haven't you?' Verity soothed. 'Until the winner is announced, there's still hope.'

'Hope?' Her father gave a disgusted snort.

'Sure. The Government might prefer a Melbourne company,' she said brightly. 'Or Hammond's partner might not pass scrutiny by the Government. You know how particular they are about any possible criminal element. It might fall through yet...anything could happen. You just have to proceed with your own bid, and keep hoping.'

He reached for her hand and gave it a squeeze. 'Oh, I won't be lying down, I can promise you that. I intend to fly up to Sydney and find out more about this overseas company. I certainly intend to find out who it is!'

'Well, don't worry about it now. Drink your coffee and get ready to go to your polo game. Mark and I are coming too.'

'You are?' He looked surprised—and pleased. 'Well, we can all drive there together in the Mercedes.'

Verity bit her lip. 'You're not...going with Tom?'

'No, I'm driving myself. Tom's already left with the horses. So...you'll come with me?'

She sighed and nodded. She had intended driving Mark in her own car and leaving the game early, giving them time to have a leisurely ride later at home, but in the light of the blow her father had just suffered she changed her mind. 'Good idea. What time are you leaving?'

Lorenzo glanced at his watch. 'Hell! Is that the time? Be ready in fifteen minutes!' He released her hand and hauled himself out of his chair. 'See you at the car!'

# CHAPTER SEVEN

A HUGE crowd had gathered at the Bloomfields' magnificent property to watch the polo match, and at the same time to enjoy the picnic atmosphere and the chance to socialise. Amy, one of the Bloomfield women, had taken Verity under her wing.

'Your friend plays well,' Amy applauded as Mark pelted a long ball down the field. 'And your father...I've never seen him play with such vigour.'

'No, nor have I,' Verity said drily. Lorenzo was playing like a man possessed, his fury at Jack Hammond's unexpected revival bringing out the fiery best in him. And no doubt Mark's expertise on the field was firing him up even further.

'Does your father always play like this?' Mark asked her when she joined him briefly between chukkas.

'Not always,' she admitted, adding with a sigh, 'His good humour this morning was short-lived, I'm afraid. He's in a foul mood...didn't you notice in the car?'

'Is it me?' Mark asked with a mocking lift of his brow. 'What's the problem? Afraid his Yankee house guest is going to run off with his daughter?'

Verity's heart turned a slow somersault. 'Is that what you're thinking of doing?' she asked, adopting a bantering tone to match his.

Mark ran a hand across his jaw. 'Don't think it's not tempting,' he drawled after a pause, his smoky gaze flicking back to the field before she could even begin to read what its depths might reveal. 'They want me for another chukka. Excuse me.'

The light in her eyes faded as he swung away. He was only tempted? Nothing more?

Lunch was an informal affair, with some visitors spreading out picnic lunches on the grass, others helping themselves to the array of delicacies provided by the local polo club. Amy dragged Verity over to a table under one of the shady umbrellas. It was a mild September day with barely a breeze, cool when the sun slipped behind the clouds but for the most part warm and sunny, a perfect day for the occasion. Her father and Mark joined them, Lorenzo red-faced and slightly breathless after his morning chukkas.

'You look as if you've had enough for one day,' Verity chided with a smile. 'I'm sure Mark's had enough too.' She was hoping Lorenzo might decide to leave early—giving her time for a leisurely horse ride with Mark before dinner.

'Rubbish, we're just warming up. After a rest and something to eat we'll be raring to go. Your friend has barely worked up a sweat.'

'His name's Mark, Daddy,' she gritted through her smile. How thankful she was for Mark's presence and Amy's bright company over lunch! Her father was grumpy and uncommunicative, still plainly preoccupied with the frustrating news he'd heard earlier in the day. And Mark's skill on the field, she suspected, hadn't improved his humour.

'Something seems to be bugging your father,' Mark commented in an undertone as Lorenzo rose to talk to someone passing by.

'He had some bad news this morning,' Verity admitted. 'It quite ruined his good mood. It's convinced him he's lost the casino bid. He's never wanted anything so badly. It's really hitting him hard.'

'I see.' Something in Mark's tone made her look up into his face, and what she glimpsed in his eyes puzzled her. A glint, a flash of steel in the grey, quickly banished as her eyes met his. 'Why is that? Your father... likes to gamble?' he hazarded.

Did Mark disapprove of gambling? Was that why his eyes had glittered with that look of... what had it been? Contempt? Satisfaction?

'Daddy's no gambler,' she assured him quickly. 'That's why he'd be so good for the casino. He'd see that it was run properly... honestly. My father might be a real bear at times,' she conceded, 'but he has no evil vices, despite what you might have heard. He's incorruptible, a man of integrity. He's always been as honest and straight as a die.'

Mark made no comment for a second, his face closed, a remote expression in his eyes. Was he unconvinced? As he caught her eye, his gaze softened, the taut muscles of his face relaxing. 'You think gambling is evil?' he asked, his tone faintly teasing now.

Verity shook her head, a hint of a smile touching her lips. 'Of course not. I quite like having a mild flutter when I go up to Jupiters, or to Wrest Point. I'm just saying that the people who run a casino must be incorruptible... totally trustworthy, above suspicion.'

'I couldn't agree more.' He reached for her hand and pressed it with a gentleness he hadn't shown before. And when she glanced up into his face again, the eyes that met hers this time were warm, almost tender. She felt her heart flutter, take flight.

'Ready for another chukka, Doctor?'

Mark plucked his gaze away from hers. 'Ready if you are, Mr Danza.'

'Then let's go!'

Dusk was falling when they drove through the gates of Tarmaroo. Lorenzo had asked Verity to drive, settling himself into the front seat beside her so that Mark was forced to sit in the seat behind. Conversation had quickly petered out. Lorenzo, obviously worn out by his strenuous exertions and in no mood anyway, Verity suspected, to make polite chit-chat with Mark or anyone else with so much on his mind, let his head slump on to his chest, and his two fellow passengers, not wanting to disturb him, fell silent too. Verity needed all her concentration anyway, as the shadows lengthened, to negotiate the winding forest road.

As she pulled up outside the house Lorenzo woke up with a grunt. While he was heaving himself out of the car Verity turned to Mark with a regretful smile.

'A bit late to go out for a ride now—even if you could face mounting a horse again today,' she said, sighing as she glanced up at the darkening sky, reluctantly abandoning her plans to take him out riding, and the chance to have him to herself for a while. If her father hadn't insisted on staying on at the Bloomfields' for drinks after the match—deliberately, she was sure, to stretch the day out—they would have been back in plenty of time. 'Maybe in the morning,' she added enticingly.

'Sure, why not?' said Mark, so carelessly that she turned away, clamping her teeth down on her lip. Didn't he *care* that they were never alone, just the two of them?

Georgia had just come in herself, and Dee, knowing they'd all had a long day and wouldn't be wanting a formal dinner, had prepared a hearty beef and vegetable casserole and a bowl of fluffy rice, which they ate informally in the morning-room off the kitchen.

'Ready for that game of snooker, Mr Danza?' Mark asked, leaning back in his chair. Despite the easy smile on his lips, there was a glitter of challenge in his grey eyes. Verity could have throttled him. She'd had something cosier in mind...something for just the two of them to do together, alone.

'Daddy, you must be worn out after the way you played today,' she put in quickly. 'Why don't you have an early night? Your snooker game can wait until——'

'It'll have to,' Lorenzo cut in. 'I'm expecting visitors—nearly forgot. Those people who've moved into the Morgans' old property—the Hendersons. Nice young couple. I met them this afternoon. They're popping in around eight to meet you and Georgia.' He shrugged his great shoulders as he rose from his chair. 'We'll have coffee when they arrive, then I'll bow out. I have some phone calls to make. You three won't mind looking after them, will you?'

Verity heaved a deep, quivering sigh. 'Oh, Daddy, what a night to invite people over—after a long day at the polo! And Georgia's had a long day too. Can't you see she just wants to relax?' *Can't you see that I want to relax too—alone with Mark?*

'It will be relaxing for her. They want to ask her about a pony for their daughter. What could be more relaxing than horse talk? What's wrong with you?' growled Lorenzo, scowling at her. 'If you're so tired out you'd better go to bed!'

'I'm not tired out,' she grated. 'But it'll mean freshening up and getting changed and——'

'Rubbish! It's just an informal visit—they're only coming over for coffee and a chat.'

Verity looked appealingly at Mark.

'You look fine,' he said, a whimsical smile on his lips, his grey eyes impassive.

She found herself clenching and unclenching the fists in her lap. Was Mark simply humouring her father, knowing full well what he was up to, that he was trying to keep the two of them from getting too close, from being thrown too much together? Or didn't Mark *want* to get too close? He was certainly showing no sign of wanting her all to himself!

She felt a wave of despondency wash over her. The one man—the *first* man she had ever seriously wanted—and he didn't seem to want *her*. Oh, it was ironic, unfair!

She slept in later than usual, exhausted physically and emotionally after finally falling asleep not long before dawn. It hadn't been a late night—she was in bed before midnight—but the evening had been trying, with no chance of a moment alone with Mark, and after bidding Mark and Georgia goodnight, she hadn't been able to sleep, tossing in her bed for hour after hour, tormented by the doubts and uncertainties clawing at her mind. Didn't Mark care about her at all?

She groaned when she reached for her watch and saw the time. Almost nine o'clock! By the time she'd showered and dressed it would be time for breakfast. She'd had thoughts of dragging Mark out for an early morning ride.

Never mind. The whole day still lay ahead of them. And today, she vowed, was going to be *her* day. Her day alone with Mark.

When she hastened into the conservatory for breakfast shortly after nine, nobody was there. The others, surely, couldn't have slept in too? As she was debating whether to give Mark a call or just wait there for him, Dee popped her head round the door.

'Your father said to tell you he's gone back to town. He didn't want to wake you to say goodbye.'

'He's gone back already?' Verity's heart gave a gleeful leap, then as quickly plunged. 'And Mark?' she asked in sudden apprehension. Surely her father hadn't persuaded Mark to go back with him! Was Dee about to hand her a note from Mark? A note saying thanks, and goodbye? Her heart swooped to her toes.

'Dr Bannister went out to the stables with Georgia.'

As relief swirled through her—relief followed by a sharp ache inside—she heard voices and laughter, and a second later Georgia strode in ahead of Mark, her tanned face glowingly alight. From the brisk morning air, Verity wondered hopefully, or... from something else? Her throat constricted as she saw Mark in the doorway, his thick brown hair tumbled and windblown, his shirt gaping open at the throat, with beads of sweat visible on the lightly tanned skin. His thigh-hugging jeans were thrust into long riding boots, his shirt-sleeves rolled up to reveal the taut muscles of his arms. Under his heavy brows his grey eyes shone like polished pewter, and his square-jawed face held a healthy glow that suggested——

'You've been out riding?' The question came out as a croak, disappointment piercing her that he hadn't waited for her to take him out.

It was Georgia who answered, 'Mark mentioned that you'd promised him a ride, so I asked if he'd like to come out with me now, while he had the chance—knowing you were planning a drive to the coast after breakfast. We expected you to join us.' Her tone was faintly defensive, her hazel eyes anxious.

'I slept in,' Verity confessed, squeezing her hands into fists and digging her fingernails into her flesh in self-recrimination. 'I'm... glad Georgia looked after you,' she said, her gaze fluttering back to Mark. He was smiling in that crooked way of his, showing no sign of compunction or regret. 'Did you have a good ride?' she asked, forcing the words out.

'Fantastic. Like the polo game yesterday, it brought back memories... great memories, of brisk gallops back on the family ranch.'

She gulped. If only she'd woken earlier, he might have had different memories by now... memories of *her*, riding along at his side... of shared smiles, meaningful glances. Would he take away memories of Georgia instead?

Stifling a groan, she said valiantly, 'Good, I'm glad.' Then in sudden doubt, 'You do still want to drive to the coast today?' Just the two of us, her eyes pleaded with him. Not that Georgia would expect to come with them. She gave riding classes on Sundays, and prospective buyers often called in, the couple from last night being two who were already expected.

'It should be lovely around Port Campbell,' she added enticingly, glancing up at the sky, where the clouds of yesterday had all but disappeared, with the sun already ablaze above the trees. At least the weather was doing its best for her!

'I'm looking forward to it,' Mark said, and though the look he gave her was unfathomable, he sounded as if he meant it. But did he mean he was looking forward to seeing the Port Campbell coastline in all its rugged beauty, or being alone with her for the day?

What did it matter? Lifting a slender hand, Verity dragged her fingers through her mane of silky black hair. He was coming!

'Let's go in, then... you must be ravenous,' she said, preferring not to think about her own appetite, her own hunger... for him.

'I'll just go and clean up a bit first. Be with you in five minutes.' He swung away, and Verity found her gaze savouring the panther-like grace of his body, the careless roll of his hips, his fluid stride.

'Did you know your father's gone back to town?' Georgia asked her.

Verity tugged her mesmerised gaze away from Mark's retreating form. 'Yes, Dee told me. Why the sudden rush to go back, do you know?' So much of a rush that he hadn't even waited around to say goodbye to her! 'Did Gloria summon him?' she asked, her lip twitching.

'I don't think Gloria's top priority at the moment,' Georgia said with a grin. 'He was mumbling something about his casino bid.'

'Oh, that.' Verity grimaced. 'He's been like a bear with a sore head ever since he heard that Hammond had come back into the race. Did he say what he intended to do?'

'I think he's on his way to Sydney. I heard him booking a flight before he left.'

Alarmed, Verity said, 'You don't think he's planning to confront Hammond?'

'Oh, I wouldn't think he'd be that stupid.'

'Maybe not. But if I know my father he'll be trying to ferret out more details about Hammond's bid, trying to find out how sound it is, and if this overseas company he's joined up with is as trustworthy as they say.'

'Well, nobody can blame a man for checking out his opposition,' said Georgia. 'There's a lot at stake. The casino's a prize everybody wants.'

'I'll be glad when it's all decided,' Verity said with a heartfelt sigh. 'Then maybe the contenders can settle down and concentrate on something else.'

'The losers, you mean,' Georgia said with a rueful twist of her lips. 'Is your father a good loser?'

'I'm not sure—in this case. He's had his heart set on building Melbourne's first casino for years. And now the chance has come at last, and it looks as if he's going to see it slip through his fingers, into the hands of a Sydney company. A company who've managed to tie themselves up with some high-flyer from overseas with money to burn. I know what he's hoping, of course...' Verity bit her lip. 'That he can expose them as crooks!'

'You think they could be?' Georgia's lovely hazel eyes widened.

Verity sighed. 'I'm sure the Government would have already checked them out thoroughly,' she said prosaically. 'Look, if Daddy loses the bid—well, too bad.

It won't be the end of the world.' She didn't want to stand around talking about casinos. She wanted to get the day under way... her first day alone—wonderfully alone—with Mark!

'Nearly there,' said Verity as they caught a fleeting glimpse of the Southern Ocean before it was blotted out by another tract of dense rainforest. Much of the Otway Forest was an impenetrable jungle, a tangle of luxuriant tree ferns and towering mountain ashes and pines and giant myrtle beech trees, in places so thick and tall that the sun seldom penetrated.

'We're lucky it's fine today,' she remarked. 'This is one of the wettest spots in Victoria. They say it rains for half the year and the trees drip for the other half, and that's not far from the truth!'

The narrow road had been twisting and turning for the past hour, dipping and rising as it cut its way through the timbered hills, over bridges and creeks, through damp fern gullies and forests of myrtle beech and blackwoods, at times bursting out of the thick forest into cleared green valleys and areas of farmland, where contented cows and sheep barely raised their heads as they passed. At times their progress was slowed by logging trucks carrying felled timber to the sawmills, but they met few other vehicles.

Now, as they drew nearer the coast, the thick forest gave way at last to bald rounded hills dotted with tight scrubby bushes.

All the while she was aware of Mark at her side, showing a keen interest in everything he saw, but he was quieter than she had ever known him. She felt her insides churning, tingling with anticipation... or was it apprehension? Did he want to be here with her, or did he wish he were somewhere else? With Georgia perhaps? Or pitting his will against her father?

The road flattened out, stretching ahead in a long straight line. They were running parallel with the sea now, though all they could see from the road was a vast expanse of barren flatness on either side and a narrow strip of blue water beyond.

'Pretty dreary countryside just along here,' she apologised, and Mark stirred at her side, seeming to emerge from some deep thoughts of his own.

'It reminds me of the moors of England,' he said slowly. 'Desolate, flat, not a tree in sight, just low stunted heathlands.'

She glanced at him. 'You never feel homesick?' she asked, then wished she hadn't. She didn't want him deciding to hightail it back to England, on the other side of the world!

'Homesick for England? No.' He didn't even need time to consider. 'I don't have particularly glowing memories of my time in England.'

His sister...his father's rejection...his parents' divorce. No wonder.

'But before your sister died,' she ventured. 'You must have *some* fond memories of your childhood. One's earliest memories—even if it's only a flash here, a flash there—can be so vivid. You look back on them and feel all warm and nostalgic.'

'Well, yes, I guess I do have... some.' There was a whimsical note in Mark's voice now. 'The odd pleasant memory... sure.'

'Tell me,' she heard herself pleading, 'what do you remember? Your first day at school? A favourite toy? Your first train ride?'

'I remember collecting a jar full of spiders,' Mark recalled, a roguish smile touching his lips. 'I was taking them home on the tram...'

'Tram? I didn't know you had trams in England.'

'Well, maybe it was a bus. Anyway, I dropped the jar, and all the spiders spilt out and ran everywhere.'

'Oh!' she shuddered. 'What on earth did you do?'

'I left them there and got off at the next stop.'

She laughed. 'What a wicked little boy you must have been!' She swung the wheel. 'This is where we turn off.' The car was pointing towards the coast now, following a well-used track.

'The Twelve Apostles?' queried Mark, reading the signpost.

'The first of our natural wonders,' Verity told him. 'People come from all over the world to see them. They're incredible...giant pillars of rock rising from the water close to the shoreline. They used to be part of the land—jutting headlands which were eroded over the years by the force of the waves and the wind, forming arches, which in time collapsed under the pounding of the sea, leaving a free-standing rock-stack in its place.'

A short drive brought them to a fenced car park below the lookout. Two other cars and a motorbike were already there.

'Now we get out and walk,' Verity said, the wind buffeting the car as she opened her door. 'We'll need our coats.'

Wrapped up against the sharp wind, faces tingling in the stinging fresh air, they followed the headland path to the edge of the massive sandstone cliffs. There were no trees to impede their view or shelter them from the wind, only a low scrub-like growth on either side of the dirt path. A few other people were standing huddled against the wind at vantage spots, cameras raised.

'Quite a sight!' breathed Mark.

They were at the cliff edge, high above the ocean, the massive limestone cliffs falling sharply away to the crashing sea far below. Mark let his gaze flicker along the broken coastline, taking in the rugged headlands and the carved cliffs and the swirls of white froth where the breakers were relentlessly pounding the shore.

'The explorer Matthew Flinders described this section of the coastline as one of the most fearful he'd ever seen.' Verity had to catch her breath against the wind and shout over the roar of the breakers below.

'Looks treacherous all right.' Mark's eyes focused on a huge rock-stack jutting defiantly from the water just off shore, the incoming waves crashing against it in a froth of white. 'Under this constant battering it's no wonder the coastline keeps changing, and is so spectacular.'

Verity tugged at his sleeve. 'We can get a good view of the Twelve Apostles from over there.'

She led him along the fenced timber lookout platform which followed the cliff edge to a spot where they had a clear safe view of the famous Twelve Apostles.

'Amazing, aren't they?' she said as they stood drinking in the stark beauty of the mighty irregular-shaped rock-stacks, some squat, others rising to a point, some dwarfed by the massive size of the others, the layered limestone varying from a warm brown to a deep ochre. 'They look different each time I come...it depends on the time of day and the weather. At sunset they can be breathtaking, a glorious burnt orange...or black, silhouetted against the red sky and the silvery-gold sea. On a moonlit night they can be quite sombre, with a magic all of their own.'

Mark started counting aloud.

'You can't see all of them from this lookout,' Verity told him. 'Some are hidden behind headlands or obscured by other rock-stacks. If you read this plaque, you'll see that the cliff faces are being eroded at the rate of about two centimetres a year. They're under constant attack by the sea.'

Mark came and read over her shoulder. She could feel his breath bringing warmth to her cold cheeks, feel his coat pressing against hers as his broad shoulders sheltered her from the wind. Acutely aware of him, of how close he was, wanting with an almost suffocating longing to be even closer to him, to snuggle up against his warmth and strength, she swayed back against him, willing him to slip his arms around her.

'I'd hate to be shipwrecked along here,' he said, gazing over her shoulder at the treacherous rocks below, and she sighed as she realised his arms were going to remain firmly clasped behind his back. 'Even if you survived the wreck,' he added ruefully, 'you'd have no hope of climbing up these sheer rock-faces.'

'You'd drown,' Verity said, and shuddered. 'Even if you made it to shore, you wouldn't last long—that narrow strip of beach disappears at high tide.'

'You'd be well and truly trapped. Nasty,' Mark agreed.

'This coast isn't called the Shipwreck Coast for nothing. It's littered with wrecks.' Reluctantly she stepped away. 'Let's drive along to the next turn-off,' she suggested, moving on. 'Loch Ard Gorge is a good case in point.'

Ten minutes later they were standing close together again, gulping against the wind on the seaward cliff overlooking the mighty Loch Ard Gorge.

'You'd never think that anyone could survive down there, would you?' said Verity, looking down into the tempestuous waters below. 'And yet two people did survive when a ship called the *Loch Ard* was wrecked here. They took shelter in that cave down there, behind that small strip of beach.'

'I would have thought that cave would be flooded at high tide,' said Mark, the wind snatching at his words and whipping them away.

'They were lucky. Want to go down and take a closer look?'

'You can get down there?'

'They've built wooden steps leading all the way down to the beach. As long as you're prepared for a long steep climb back up,' she challenged him.

'Lead on. The exercise will do us good—if it doesn't kill us first.'

On their way down, using the rail for support as they followed the steep, winding descent, they met one other couple labouring up, but when they finally stepped on to the sandy beach at the bottom, they found they were alone. They felt dwarfed by the encircling cliffs, the wind whipping at their hair and clothes as they stood at the shoreline watching the waves tumbling on to the beach and the angry white froth swishing and swirling around the narrow entrance into the gorge.

'Want to explore the cave?' Verity asked after a while, and at a nod from Mark she turned and moved towards the rocky cliff behind, pausing at the cave's dark entrance.

'It gives you an eerie feeling,' she said, shivering as she felt Mark's hands slip over her shoulders.

'You're right.' His voice was a low rumble, close to her ear. 'I don't think I'd trust that tide not to come in and cut off our escape route.'

She could feel herself trembling, but it wasn't the thought of being trapped by the tide that was making her tremble, it was Mark's touch, and being here alone with him, just the two of them in this wild, remote, desolate spot... alone with the one man in all the world that she wanted to be with.

'Verity...'

Something in Mark's voice turned her into a quivering statue.

# SHATTERED WEDDING 121

'Hell, Verity...' He seized her by the shoulders and swung her round to face him.

Her eyes leapt to his. 'Mark?' His name was a husky whisper. She sensed a struggle going on within him...was confused, shaken by the wildness, the torment she saw in his eyes.

'Damn it,' he muttered hoarsely, curving his fingers under her chin. He bent his head and brushed his lips to hers...lightly, testingly...one kiss, then another, then another, with each touch gradually increasing the pressure, the exquisite suspense.

Her eyelids fluttered closed, a hot flame licking through her each time his lips touched hers. Instinctively, as his mouth lingered longer the next time, she let her lips soften under his, moving them in sensual invitation.

He drew back sharply.

Her eyelashes flew upward. She caught a dark, agonised spark in his eyes a split second before he groaned and dragged her savagely against him, his mouth coming down to crush hers, his lips searing, devouring, aflame with hunger, as if those testing kisses, the sweet taste of her lips, had unlocked something inside him, something he had been keeping rigidly under control.

He dragged his lips away only long enough to gasp, 'I've been fighting this, fighting *you*, Verity, but I'm damned if I can fight fate!' before his mouth captured hers again, his lips fiercely ravishing as they ground over hers, his arms tight bands around her soft slenderness, pressing her pliant body hard against his muscular strength as if he would never let her go.

Even when they finally surfaced for air, he didn't release her, drawing tiny gasps from her as his burning mouth attacked her cheeks, her eyes, her jaw, her throat in a frenzy of new, feverish kisses. As her heartbeat skyrocketed, she was dimly conscious of him mumbling something against the softness of her skin in a low agonised moan, words that sounded like, 'This is impossible... it's impossible!'

No, it's not, Verity cried back soundlessly, her senses spinning in dizzy happiness as she clutched at his shoulders and clawed at his hair, straining her body against him to show just how possible it was. It's happening... and you want it as much as I do!

Minutes later some sound or sixth sense must have warned them that they were no longer alone, and reluctantly, with tiny moans of regret, they pulled apart at last, loosening their grip on each other, yet still unwilling to let go altogether. Glancing round, they saw two young men in black leather trudging across the sand, bemused grins on their lips.

'Time to go?' Mark's tone was rueful as he swung her round and steered her towards the steps.

She wondered if he was already regretting his feverish kisses, his loss of control—hadn't he groaned that it was impossible?—but as they toiled up the timber steps he stayed close and kept his arm round her all the way, his fingers firm round her waist so that she could feel their heat even through her soft padded jacket. And he kept glancing down at her and smiling with a tenderness, a passion he had never revealed to her before.

Blissfully she smiled back, showing her own feelings only too plainly, wanting him to know precisely how she felt, and that *she* didn't believe anything was impossible.

When they finally reached the car and collapsed into their seats, he sat looking at her for a long aching moment, then he pulled her into his arms again and pressed his lips fiercely to hers. But only for a moment this time... he drew back almost at once, a determined glint in his eye, his hands gripping her shoulders so tightly that she almost cried out.

'I can't let you go now,' he said. 'I won't!'

'Mark...' She looked up at him, her eyes, even as they shimmered with joy, faintly puzzled at his vehemence. 'I don't want you to let me go...can't you tell? Why should you have to? Why did you say it was impossible?'

He didn't answer for a moment, his fingers biting deeper into her flesh. Searching his eyes in sudden fear, she saw conflicting emotions warring in the grey depths, pain and passion and other intense emotions she couldn't read.

Finally, as she waited in painful suspense, he seemed to come to a decision, the tense muscles of his face relaxing as he said, 'You're right. Nothing's impossible, if you want something enough. Hell, if I want it! You and I, Verity...it's no use fighting what's between us. We both sensed it, knew it, right from the start, didn't we? Well, I did.'

'You did?' She gazed at him in awed disbelief. Had he been fighting it, struggling against his feelings all this time? *Why*? Was it the memory of his disastrous marriage that had held him back? Was he afraid to trust a woman again, to trust his own feelings? She wanted to cry out that she understood. Hadn't she suffered a similar blow, and emerged from it?

Her lips burst into a smile. She would prove to Mark that he could trust her, if he would only give her the chance. She loved him so much that she knew she would follow him anywhere...even to America, if he decided ultimately to go back. Her father would just have to accept it.

Could that be another thing, perhaps, that had been holding him back?

'Verity...' Mark brushed silky strands of black hair from her eyes with infinite gentleness. 'I know it's too soon, far too soon. It must seem impossible that it could happen so quickly...' Was *that* what he'd meant when he'd said it was impossible? 'But I love you, Verity—I can't hold it back any longer. I love you... and I can't, I *won't* let you slip out of my life now.'

She couldn't believe she was hearing the words... but as she gazed, stunned, into his eyes, she knew that he meant them, knew that they were true.

'I love you too,' she breathed, the admission leaping unbidden to her lips. 'It happened the same way for me. I—I didn't think it was possible either. To feel what I do... to know so quickly. There was a time when I thought I'd never trust another man.'

She smiled shyly up at him. 'And yet Daddy too... that's how it was when he met my mother. They both fell in love at first sight. They just knew. He's never loved another woman since.'

Something had changed—she sensed it immediately. She saw it in the tightening of his jaw, in the flatness, the remoteness that came into his eyes. She wished she'd kept her father's name out of it. Mark knew full well that her father wasn't happy about their friendship, and she knew it must be frustrating, hurtful for him. But surely, once Lorenzo knew how Mark felt about her, and how she felt about him...

'Verity...' Mark's grip tightened on her shoulders. 'I'm not interested in having an affair. I want to marry you. I want you to be my wife.'

As she gasped, he released his grip on one shoulder and pressed a finger to her lips. 'I don't want you to answer me now, or to feel that I'm in any way rushing you, or pressuring you. You don't have to say anything now. I just want you to know what I have in mind... what my intentions are.' His lip curved into a wry smile, as if he were apologising for being old-fashioned.

He wanted her to be his wife... he was asking her to marry him. Dazed, she let the words spin round in her head as he went on, his voice low, intense, his eyes burning into hers.

'But I don't want to shilly-shally around with a long courtship. I don't want an engagement lasting weeks or months. I want you for my wife, Verity, and I want us to start living our lives together as soon as we can. Time is too precious to waste. In one week from now I'm going to want your answer, Verity. And if it's yes, I'll want to get married as soon as we can arrange it.'

Smiling with a piercing tenderness, he looked down into her dazed eyes. 'Sure, I know we haven't known each other long, and sure, we still have a lot to learn about each other. But if we're both sure of our feelings, and *I* am, nothing—*nothing*,' he repeated, and there was an intensity, an impatience in his voice that he couldn't hide, 'need hold us back. We'll have the rest of our lives to discover all there is to know about each other.'

Verity nodded, obediently saying nothing, but her eyes were nakedly revealing, telling him without the need for words that she agreed with everything he'd said.

'Now, let's just enjoy the rest of our day... the rest of this week.' Mark's voice was gentle now as he gave her arm a squeeze, the urgent pressure of his fingers belying his coolness, revealing that he was more tense, more fraught with emotion than he appeared. 'Do you think we could stay down here at Tarmaroo for a couple of extra days?'

She looked up at him and smiled. 'Oh, yes, Mark, of course. That sounds wonderful. Mark...' She bit her lip, her hand involuntarily fluttering upward to thread her fingers through her long hair. 'Mark, I'm hungry,' she said.

It broke the tension. She could see him visibly relaxing. 'Let's drive into Port Campbell,' she suggested, 'and find somewhere to eat.'

# CHAPTER EIGHT

THE next three days flew by in a blissful, euphoric whirl. They spent all their waking hours together, riding, helping Georgia around the stud, going for long drives, exploring the forest and the volcanic lakes and much of the rugged south coast.

They stole quiet moments alone together whenever they could, losing themselves in each other's arms in an ecstasy of kisses and intimate caresses, yet never going beyond a certain point. Mark insisted on it, and on sleeping apart at night, not wanting, Verity suspected, to give her father any chance to put objections in their path, should he happen to find out that they were sleeping together and accuse Mark of emotional blackmail.

Perhaps, too, it was Mark's way of not putting any pressure on her, of not wanting heady emotion to sway her decision. Or maybe he just wanted the timing to be right, with no guilt, no subterfuge, no hole-and-corner fumbling to spoil their ultimate union.

During those three days and evenings they talked about many things—about their interests and their innermost beliefs and their opinions on a whole range of subjects, but they didn't talk much about their families, or dwell on the past. Verity sensed that Mark was keen to look ahead, not back.

On Wednesday morning they drove back to town along the scenic Great Ocean Road, hugging the coast all the way to Anglesey beach, where they branched off to rejoin the main highway to Geelong, stopping for a seafood lunch at a harbourside restaurant in Geelong before driving on to the city.

'Mark... you'll be able to meet my brother Johnny soon—and I *know* you'll like each other,' Verity said as they hit the city traffic. 'He's due home next month.' By which time, she mused, quivering at the thought, she and Mark would be planning their wedding-day. Because she *was* going to say 'yes'. She'd known that from the moment he'd asked.

'I'll look forward to meeting him,' Mark said, but his voice sounded oddly remote. Was he afraid that Johnny would be against their marriage—as her father was bound to be?

'This weekend,' he went on smoothly—had he deliberately switched to another topic? 'I'd like to start looking for a house.'

Instantly she forgot Johnny. *This weekend*, she thought dreamily. When he pops the question again—and will demand my answer. She gulped, a light-headedness sweeping over her. Once she said yes, they could start looking for a house together...a family home like Tarmaroo, only *theirs*, their very own. And closer to the city for their work.

She left Mark in the Tower car park, she going one way, he another, promising to meet again in an hour for dinner. When she reached her apartment, she flicked on her answering machine and flopped into an armchair, kicking off her shoes as she tore open her mail.

The first few telephone messages weren't important. She jotted down a couple of phone numbers, then tensed suddenly in her chair.

'Ring me the second you come in.' It was her father's voice. 'We need to talk. I've been trying to reach you all day.'

He sounded irate. Furious. What was it all about? Georgia—or Dee—must have told him that Mark had stayed on at Tarmaroo until today, and mentioned how close, how inseparable they had been. Well, so what? she thought rebelliously. I'll tell him how I feel about Mark and he can like it or lump it.

She hauled herself out of her chair and stomped across to the phone, running the tip of her tongue over her lips as she picked up the receiver.

Her father answered at the first ring. 'Danza.' His tone was terse.

'Daddy, I——'

'Where are you? Home?'

'Yes, I just——'

'Come up here. Now!' He cut her off.

Gritting her teeth, she spent a moment composing herself, then slammed out, catching the lift up to the next floor.

At her knock her father jerked open the door and dragged her inside, his huge frame shaking with rage. 'I was right all along. I knew it. I knew we couldn't trust him!'

Her heart banged in her chest. 'Who are you talking about? Jack Hammond?' she hazarded, knowing it was a vain hope. Dee or Georgia must have let something drop about her closeness to Mark. And her father had at once jumped to all the wrong conclusions, casting Mark in the role of wicked seducer. She clenched her fists, ready to do battle.

'No, not Hammond, damn it!' Her father's eyes blazed. 'But he's involved in this...they're both involved. Hammond and this shining knight of yours!'

Her heart quailed in sudden fear. 'You mean...Mark?'

'You know damned well that's who I mean. He's played you for a fool, and me too. He's *used* you to get close to me!'

The world seemed to spin and then stop—and her heart with it. Through a fog of doubt and apprehension, she demanded shakily, 'Involved in...what? Daddy, what has Mark done?'

'He's snatched the casino from under my nose—that's what he's done! He's joined forces with Hammond!'

'What?' She stared at him, the blood draining from her cheeks. 'I don't believe it!'

'Oh, it's true all right. I found out while I was up in Sydney this week. Dr Mark Bannister—our smooth-talking house guest—is the one who's financing Hammond. His company has formed a consortium with Hammond's to make sure they win the casino bid. Ask him, if you don't believe me! Ask him if he owns Carson Investments. Ask him if his stepfather's name was Sam Carson.'

*Sam...* Verity drew in a tremulous breath, her shoulders slumping. She felt as if she had been kicked in the stomach. 'But Mark wouldn't—he couldn't—he would have told me!'

Her father smiled grimly. 'Well, now you know the kind of man he is. I did try to warn you...'

'I need to...think.' She swung away from him, almost falling as a giddiness swept over her. Her father caught her arm.

'Here...sit down. I'll pour you a drink.'

'No.' She set her jaw, fighting the giddiness until it passed. 'I'm going to see Mark. I *was* intending to have dinner with him, but now...' In a black cloud of despair, she made for the door, summoning her flagging energy to move one leg stiffly after the other. 'I have to give him the chance to explain...'

Her father followed her to the lift, his face drawn now, anxious. 'Do you need to hear any more? Do you need him to spell it out? He's conned us, pet. He wormed his way into our lives just to find out what he'd be up against...no doubt hoping to find some ammunition to use against me to spoil *my* bid. Has he been asking questions about me? About my business? About *anything*?'

Her stricken face gave him his answer. Mark's interest in her father, his probing into Lorenzo's honesty, the antagonism she had sensed in him... it all made sense now. Mark and her father were business rivals! Mark *had* conned them. He *had* used her. Right from the very beginning. She'd always half suspected he had known who she was when they first met. He'd just been using her all along! Nothing he said, no amount of explaining, could change that!

'Thank your lucky stars you've found out in time,' Lorenzo growled, his big hand stroking her shoulder. 'Before you got any more involved with him... before you lost your heart to him. Or anything else.' He looked at her sharply. 'He hasn't——?'

'No!' The denial was torn from her. Had Mark known that he would be exposed eventually? Was that why he hadn't made love to her? Because some spark of humanity, some grain of consideration, had stopped him from going that far? Because deep down he'd felt guilty about what he was doing, about deceiving her, using her, conning her and her family?

But he'd asked her to marry him! His love, his feeling for her, had seemed so genuine. She turned away with a groan, and stumbled into the open lift. Had all that been a sham too, a ploy to pull the wool over her eyes? Could he be that evil, that cunning, that *low*? She couldn't believe it, even now, even after what she'd just learnt about him... That wasn't the man she had come to know, the man who had revealed so many fine qualities, the man she had come to love—and still loved. Yes, she did still love him, she realised, sick to the stomach as she felt. What kind of fool did that make her?

She had to have it out with him!

\* \* \*

# SHATTERED WEDDING 131

When Mark opened the door of his hotel room at her urgent knock, she pushed past him, grim-lipped, without waiting for an invitation, not caring if he was half dressed, or busy, or with anybody else.

'Verity! What is it? What's wrong?' He had seen at once the mood she was in, and knew that she hadn't simply come early for their dinner date. She was still wearing the blouse and trousers she'd been wearing all day.

She swung round to face him, her pent-up fury and anguish spilling out. 'You lied to me! You've *used* me... from the first moment we met! You fooled all of us! I—I can't believe it! You... and Hammond... joining forces to steal the casino bid from my father!'

Mark's mouth tightened. Under his dark brows his eyes hardened. Almost as if he, not she, were the one in the right, the one with a grievance. A muscle twitched at his jaw, the only sign of any emotion.

'So...' he said at length, his hand lifting with that tigerish grace that was so distinctively his, and hanging for a moment in the air, mesmerising her even now. 'I take it that my involvement with Hammond, which was supposed to be kept strictly quiet, has been leaked somehow.'

His tone was cold, without expression. Not a sign of embarrassment, or regret, or discomfort, she noted dully, and that was what hurt most of all.

'Who ferreted it out? Your father?' There was raking scorn in his voice, as if her father, not he, deserved the blame.

'It's true?' she croaked. Why was she even asking— he'd just admitted it, hadn't he? Suddenly he was a stranger to her.

'Yes, it's true.' His eyes were like glacial ice, as wintry as his tone. 'But it has nothing to do with you and me, Verity. It's a business matter. I signed up with Hammond while I was up in Sydney for those few days before the medical conference... before we even met.'

'But you've gone ahead with it!' She swung her face away with a whimper of hurt. Gathering her flagging strength for another attack, she spun back to face him, her pained eyes shooting violet sparks. 'You've still gone ahead—knowing how much my father wants the casino licence himself! Why would *you* want it? A casino!'

His lips settled into a tight smile, but there was no humour in it, or in his eyes. 'It's a prize many people want, Verity. You're saying your father deserves it above everybody else?'

'That's not what I meant! It's the way you—the way you just stood by while I told you how much it meant to my father, and you said nothing, did nothing, didn't even mention that you were in the race yourself—not even when I told you how upset my father was over Hammond now looking the likely winner!'

'It wasn't appropriate.' He was unmoved, his tone implacable. 'There was no need to involve you in our fight, Verity. There still isn't.'

'You mean... even though we *know* now, you still intend to go on with it—supporting Hammond against my father?' She stared at him in disbelief. 'Even though a few days ago you asked me to marry you? Even though, if I were to accept, my father would become your—your father-in-law?'

A shadow, a darkness, swept across his face. 'A pledge is a pledge, Verity. It's business—cold hard business. It won't affect my relationship with you.' She expected him to add 'or your father', but he didn't. Did he believe that was too much to hope for?

'But why all the secrecy in the first place?' She still didn't understand. 'Why did you ask Hammond to keep your name quiet after you'd signed up?' She bit her lip, her heart sinking. Was it as her father had said... so that he could worm his way, through *her*, into the Danza family's confidence, and size up his opposition?

'It's not an unusual request.' Mark's tone was dismissive. 'Other contenders have kept their names secret from the Press as well. I'm a doctor first and foremost, Verity. I preferred to let Hammond be the public face. After all, he's the one who'll be building and running the casino. I'll only be providing the long-running finance. And a lot of jobs, I hope.'

'But you didn't mind *Hammond* coming out in public and talking openly about the consortium!'

'As long as my name wasn't made public—no. There had been rumours that Hammond was going under. The Press were sniffing around, making damaging allegations. It was threatening Hammond's reputation—and his bid. The only way he could put the rumours to rest was to go public and admit that he'd formed a consortium with another company, an overseas company with solid finance and an impeccable reputation. He wasn't obliged to name the company he'd signed up with. Only the casino authorities needed to know.'

She looked up at him, her hurt eyes appealing to him. 'But couldn't you have told *us*? My father might not have liked it—but he would have respected you for being honest about it.'

'The successful bidder still hasn't been announced,' Mark reminded her, his tone cold again, uncompromising, unmoved by her plea on her father's behalf. 'Your father and I are competitors, Verity. It wouldn't have been appropriate to discuss it with your father at this delicate stage. Particularly as I was seeing his daughter.'

'You could pull out!' she cried recklessly. 'If you really loved me, you would!' Her father no longer believed he had any chance of winning the bid... not with the terms that Hammond, with Mark's help, was now able to offer the Government.

'I do really love you, Verity, but I can't do that. I've made a commitment, and it's binding. It's business, Verity——'

'You're as hard-boiled as my father!' she accused, her cheeks flushed with hurt anger.

'In matters of business, one needs to be. I'm not hard-boiled when it comes to my asthma patients. Or to you...' His tone softened, caressing her, weakening her defences. 'Put it out of your mind, Verity. As I said before, it's nothing to do with you and me.' The steely glint in his eye was implacable, but, even so, she made one last attempt to sway him.

'It is, if it causes bad blood between you and my father—the two men I love most in the——' She clamped the rest off, drawing in her breath as she realised what she had revealed, prematurely, three days too early. Yet at the same time she knew that it was true, she did love Mark—even the shock of today's revelations couldn't stop her loving him—so what did it matter if she confessed it now? It would take more than a bit of business rivalry between Mark and her father to kill the love she felt for him.

At once she saw the expression in his eyes change, the hardness giving way to tenderness, and relief. 'You're saying...you love me, Verity? That this hasn't...turned you against me?' But he still hadn't moved, still wasn't touching her, still wasn't making any attempt to take her into his arms.

She looked up at him helplessly. I'm not going to lose you, Mark, she vowed silently. Not over a lousy casino bid.

Lifting her chin, she said, 'You wouldn't let me tell you the other day, Mark, but I...I've loved you from the day I met you—though *I* tried to fight it too, at first.

And whatever you've done, whatever you do in the future——' a huskiness crept into her voice '—it won't change how I feel.'

He stood like a rock, still not saying a word, not moving a muscle, and only when she looked at him more closely did she realise he was fighting some deep emotion, a pulse beating at his temple, his jaw clenched, a silvery shimmer in his eyes.

The sight of the tension he was under plucked further admissions from her. 'I've never loved anyone before... not the way I love you, Mark. I've never felt——' She gulped, 'Mark, this time I *know*. When it's real, you do know. With Donald I... it didn't go deep. Even before I found out the kind of man he was.'

At long last she saw his lips move, saw a deep yearning stir in his eyes. 'You feel that sure? Even after this?'

She lifted her chin, her eyes moist, a sapphire blur. 'It's because I love you so much, Mark, that I... that all this... Mark, it hasn't changed how I feel. And it won't. Yes, I'm that sure.'

He moved at last, like a panther in slow motion, reaching out to her, his hands closing over her shoulders. But he held her away from him, keeping her at arm's length as his glittering eyes searched her face. 'Sure enough to go on loving me, believing in me, no matter what strains and difficulties and maybe even shocks could lie ahead of us?'

When the successful bidder was announced, did he mean? The friction that still lay ahead, between Mark and her father? She felt a tiny shiver. She would weather it... somehow. As long as she was with Mark.

Gulping, she nodded. It wasn't going to be easy, but their love and their commitment to each other would see them through.

Commitment? But they weren't actually committed yet... Did Mark still want——?

'Mark, I want to marry you and be with you always!' The words were torn from her, along with all her hopes and yearnings. She looked up at him in quick apprehension. But did he still want to marry *her*, after the doubts she had shown, the accusations she had hurled at him? 'You do still want to marry me...don't you?' she faltered.

He laughed softly, and gathered her in his arms, stroking her long hair as he held her against him, so tightly that she could barely breathe.

'Oh, yes...I do. And I accept with all my heart. And,' he added, a note of humour in his voice now, 'I look forward to telling our children how their mother couldn't wait for a formal proposal and jumped in and proposed to *me*. And it's not even a leap year!'

She blushed becomingly, and stole a look up at him, her deep blue eyes alight with a mixture of joy and relief. She caught the teasing light in his eye, and her own sense of humour stirred, prompting her to retaliate.

'And I'll look forward to telling our children that I couldn't wait forever for *you* to pop the question!'

'Hussy! Step over here...' With his arm still around her, he drew her over to the desk, where he unlocked an attaché case and drew out a small velvet-covered box. 'This is what I've been wanting to give you since I first fell in love with you,' he said, handing it to her, his eyes serious now, a silvery glow kindling in the grey depths.

He watched her face as she opened it, saw her eyes widen, a smile of delight lighting up her face as she cried, 'Oh, Mark, it's beautiful!'

'Sapphires...to match your eyes. And diamonds...because you're as precious to me as... No, you're *more* precious to me than diamonds or any stone. Far more.'

Verity gulped down a wave of emotion as Mark reached down and took the ring from its box.

'It was my mother's engagement ring,' he told her. 'Here... let me put it on your finger. If it fits, her wedding-ring will fit you too. The two were made to go together.'

'Your father gave this to your mother?' she asked as he slipped the ring on to her finger. To her delighted surprise, a perfect fit! 'Or... your stepfather?'

'No, my... real father.'

'Oh.' The father who had rejected him... who had abandoned his family after Mark's sister died. Verity was surprised that his ring would mean so much to Mark... but she could see that it did. His father must have hurt him more, meant more to him, than he had made out.

'I'll treasure it always,' she said, holding her finger up to the light. 'Oh, Mark... I'm so happy!'

The doubts and misery of a few moments ago were like a bad memory already. A memory to be squashed and put out of her mind forever. The future was what mattered now. Her future with Mark.

She only hoped her father would come around, once he knew that they were in love and planning to marry. But that could wait until tomorrow. Tonight belonged to her and Mark... just the two of them, alone together.

Mark pulled her back into his arms, his hand coming up to cup her chin, tilting her face to his. 'And now... it's time to seal our union with a kiss. The first of many... of a lifetime of kisses. A lifetime of loving.'

She trembled as his head came down, eagerly opening her lips to meet his, thinking as she became lost in his slow, drugging kisses that now she had everything she had ever wanted... the man she loved, the love she'd long dreamed about, the promise of a future she had always hoped for.

And that was as far as her conscious mind went, a dreamy euphoria sweeping over her, driving out all but the sensations running riot inside her, as Mark's kisses, the pressure of his muscular body against hers, the fiery exploration of his hands all over her body, sent her spinning into a spiral of erotic pleasure.

In the fever of the moment, she hardly noticed that he was undressing her, hardly realised that she was doing the same to him, ripping at the buttons of his shirt, dragging it from his shoulders, fumbling with the belt of his trousers, until she felt him pause, heard him groan against her hair, 'Would you rather wait, Verity? I'll stop if you want it... Only tell me now, my darling. Because if I go any further, it will be too late!'

'No... please! It's what I want! You're what I want!' She clung to him. It was already too late as far as she was concerned.

'Then let's do the right thing. Excuse me... just for a second.'

She was almost past the point of caring—if she had Mark's baby, she'd be glad, over the moon—but that wasn't what Mark meant, or not the only thing he was thinking about, and she was grateful for his concern, loving him all the more.

When he came back she heard him catch his breath at the sight of her standing naked before him, felt weak as he caught her in his arms and groaned, 'I thought you were beautiful before... but you take my breath away,' as he sank his face into the satin hollow between her breasts.

By the time he lowered her on to the fluffy carpet, she was moaning in ecstasy, whimpering with the need for release, as aroused as he, and nothing, nobody, could have stopped what happened next.

As she soared to heights she had never dreamed possible, incredibly she found herself soaring even higher, to a shuddering peak she had never reached before, had never known existed, sobbing Mark's name aloud as wave after wave of wild sensation rocketed through her.

As she writhed and moaned, she felt Mark's body arch back, and arch again, heard him gasping, 'I love you, I love you, I love you,' over and over again as he spun to heights that matched her own.

They collapsed, spent, against each other, whispering their love for each other as they lay wrapped in each other's arms, totally at one, totally fulfilled.

After a long time Verity stirred and sat up. 'I do believe I'm hungry.'

'Again?' There was a drowsy amusement in his voice. 'You're always hungry.'

She smiled at him without shyness, her face alight with her love. 'I'd better slip home first and make myself respectable.' She reached for her clothes.

He rolled over and heaved himself up on one elbow. 'Why don't we just stay here and call Room Service? I'll have some champagne sent up. Unless you particularly want to go out to celebrate?'

She shook her head. 'I'd rather stay here. Just the two of us.' Besides, if they ventured out to a restaurant, it would be just their luck to run into her father. It would be bad enough having him see them together. Worse, if he noticed she was wearing Mark's ring. Why risk him making a scene in public, and spoiling their special night? She would tell him quietly later. And once he had accepted it—*if* he did—they could celebrate officially, as a family. Johnny, she knew, would be pleased when he heard that his sister had found true love at last—with a man who, wonder of wonders, was truly in love with *her*... not with her money, not with the Danza name or what an alliance with Danza's daughter could do for him... with her for herself.

'How about a hot shower before I call Room Service?' Mark eyed her hungrily as he caught her hand and tugged her to her feet.

'You mean...' Her pulse began to pound anew.

'That's precisely what I mean.'

It was late when she left Mark's room and she was floating on air as she rode up in the family lift after kissing him goodnight in the foyer down below.

Over their champagne, and the candlelit dinner that was wheeled in for them on a trolley, they had made plans, many plans, plans she could hardly believe were happening. She had promised to marry Mark in October. Next month!

'I've waited all my life for this...for *you*,' he'd told her, with a tenderness that had melted her heart, 'and I want to start living our lives together as soon as we can arrange it. I meant what I said to you a few days ago...I want to get married straight away, as soon as we can make the necessary arrangements. The soonest date possible, by law, is a month and one day from the date we apply for a licence. We'll apply tomorrow and get married midway through next month. You'll be an October bride.'

She had smiled indulgently, touched by his impatience. 'I'd like that too, but, Mark—a month! Will that give us enough time...?'

'It will if we make it a small garden wedding. Let's get married at Tarmaroo—with just your family and closest friends. Garden weddings seem to be all the rage in this country. We'll hire a marquee, in case of rain. What do you say?'

'Oh Mark, I'd love to be married at Tarmaroo. It's a lovely idea.' She remembered something. 'Georgia has an uncle who's a civil celebrant. I'll ask him if he'll come and marry us in the garden.'

'And you're happy to make it a small wedding, with as little fuss and fanfare as possible?' He eyed her in swift concern.

She smiled, reassuring him. 'I can't think of anything worse than a lot of fuss and fanfare. We won't even put a notice in the papers. We don't want the Press clamouring for interviews and photographs and turning it into a circus.' As her engagement to Donald had fast been turning into when she had called it off. Donald, with the support of her father and his own parents, had insisted on a huge formal wedding with over two hundred guests—a big cathedral ceremony in Melbourne, with a lavish reception at the most sought-after reception house in town. Her head reeled at the memory of the planning that had been under way before she had mercifully backed out.

But even with a small informal wedding there were still plans to make, all sorts of things to decide on— what to wear, how many bridesmaids to have, who to invite. And there were the flowers and the wedding cake and the invitations...

'I'll ask Georgia to be my bridesmaid,' she decided on an impulse. 'And, Mark, let's just ring people or send hand-written notes instead of sending out printed invitations. Organising printed ones always takes time, and this way will be much more friendly and personal.'

Mark smiled, and stroked her cheek. 'Suits me. You can draw up a list and we'll get on to it in the next day or so. They might not all be able to come, but as long as you and I are there, and your family and a couple of attendants to act as witnesses...isn't that all that matters?'

She nodded, relief and happiness shining in her eyes. Mark made it all sound so simple! But there was one thing...

'I would like my brother Johnny to be there, if possible,' she told him. 'He's due to finish his course at Harvard in about three weeks...'

'Then there's no problem...is there? He'll be home in time. He does plan to come home straight away?' He'd noticed her faint frown.

'Well...he may have planned to travel round for a bit. I'm not sure.' She lifted her chin. 'No. Once he hears the news, he'll be home like a shot. He'll want to be here for my wedding.' If Johnny believed it was really going ahead this time...

She would just have to convince him.

She smiled up into Mark's face. There was so much to do, so much to plan, so much to think about. And all she wanted to think about was being in Mark's arms. Which was where she found herself a moment later, any further plans being set aside until tomorrow...when they intended to break the news to her father.

# CHAPTER NINE

'YOU'RE *what*? Are you crazy, girl? You've only known the man a week!' Her father looked ready to explode.

Verity gulped, drawing her robe more tightly around her. Her father, already fully dressed and ready for the office, had knocked on her door just as she was stepping out of the shower. He had come expecting to console her, expecting her to have broken up with Mark the previous night and to be in need of a bit of fatherly sympathy.

Instead, she had faced him defiantly, and defended Mark's stand on the casino, supporting his wish for secrecy, for wanting to keep his business life separate from his medical life and even more so from his private life...especially since he was romantically involved with the daughter of a competitor.

When her father had snorted that it was a paltry defence and she was a fool to be taken in by it, she had shown him Mark's ring and told him that they loved each other and were planning to get married.

'Tell me you didn't say that. Tell me you're pulling my leg.' Her father seized on the slim hope, his voice gruff with anxiety, his face florid with stifled rage.

'I've never meant anything more in my life, Daddy.' She threw back her head. 'I love Mark and I intend to marry him. Next month.'

She took a step back as Lorenzo's body seemed to swell, his face darkening as the explosion came.

'*Next month*?' he roared. 'You really have gone out of your mind! You intend to rush into marriage with a man we know virtually nothing about—a man who's already proved he hides things from you? For pity's sake, girl, what's got into you? Why the frantic rush? Afraid, is he,' he sneered, 'that if he delays too long, you might find out more about him and change your mind? Afraid we'll expose him for the charlatan he is before he can get his ring on your finger?'

She held on to her temper. She must stay calm, or she would never be able to reason with her father and put him qualms to rest, let alone gain his support. 'Neither of us wants to wait, Daddy. We want to start living our lives together, as soon as we can. You wouldn't want us having a hole-and-corner affair, would you... or living openly together? We want to live together as man and wife... have our own home... start a family.'

Lorenzo threw up his hands. 'Think what would have happened if you'd rushed into marriage with Donald Makim!'

'That was different! I didn't love Donald the way I love Mark. And Donald didn't love me. I know Mark loves me.' She met her father's eyes unblinkingly. 'I've never been more sure of anything in my life. Or of my love for him.'

She saw her father struggling against his fury, curbing the objections that rose to his lips, not wanting to risk having her rebel and doing something even more drastic—like running away with Mark.

'Look...' He appealed to her. 'If you insist on getting engaged to this man, at least give yourselves a few months to get to know each other. That's what engagements are for... to get to know each other before you commit your lives to each other. And I'd advise you to keep it quiet. No public announcements. We don't want the media pouncing on it, and hounding us, like they did with you and Donald.'

# SHATTERED WEDDING

At least they were in accord on that point—if for different reasons. Her father wanted to keep it quiet so that if—*when*, he would be hoping—she and Mark broke up, there would be no public scandal, no snide jeers at a second broken engagement.

'We intend to,' she said evenly. 'We'd already decided not to put an engagement notice in the paper. And we don't want a big splashy wedding, Daddy. This time it's not going to be a formal church wedding with a glittering reception to follow with hundreds of guests. Mark and I want a small, informal wedding in the garden at Tarmaroo...with only our family and very closest friends. A quiet, intimate family wedding.'

'You've discussed all this...already?' He looked shaken now. It was more serious than he'd thought.

'Well, not all the details, naturally,' she admitted. 'But we intend to keep it simple,' she warned him. 'I'd like Johnny to be there, of course. He *will* be home by early next month...won't he?'

Her father's gaze was hooded, enigmatic, as his eyes met hers. 'He'll be finished at Harvard by then—yes. But he won't be home until some time later. I have some business I want him to attend to in America before he comes home.'

Business? She frowned, her eyes narrowing. Business he'd just thought of? Was he hoping that if he delayed Johnny's return, he could delay the wedding...hoping that if he stretched the time out, she'd have longer to think about it, and be more likely to call it off?

She sucked in her breath. 'Couldn't Johnny go back to the States *after* the wedding and see to your business then?'

'No...it's something that needs attention now. In fact I was thinking of cutting his course short to deal with it.'

'It's that urgent?' she asked. 'What's up? What's wrong?'

'Nothing that need concern you.'

Normally he was open about his business dealings, keen to keep his son and daughter well-briefed on all aspects of the business in case they one day had unexpectedly to take over the reins. His evasion made her look at him sharply, a piercing suspicion flaring.

'Are you sure it doesn't concern me?' she asked, frowning. 'You're not—you wouldn't dare...' She could hardly get the words out, she was so incensed. 'If you're sending Johnny to check up on Mark...'

To her amazement, he didn't deny it. 'If you're so sure he's what he says he is,' he said, grim-lipped, 'you have nothing to worry about. It only makes sense, pet...your whole future's at stake here. I'm only trying to protect *you*...to save you from possible pain.' As she opened her mouth to protest, he held up his hand. 'Don't worry, Johnny will be discreet. Your...fiancé won't even know about it.'

'If Mark finds out I'll never forgive you,' she vowed, pressing her hands to her heaving chest. 'Daddy, I *love* him. He's the finest man I've ever met. If you do anything to spoil it——'

'He won't find out. Trust me, pet. I have only your best interests at heart. I'm not pursuing a vendetta, if that's what you think I'm doing. If your fiancé and Hammond win the casino bid in the end, then I'll have to accept it, like it or not.'

But he would be doing his best to make sure they didn't, she thought, resentment flaring. It wasn't only his daughter he wanted to protect, it was his own interests as well.

'When Mark becomes your son-in-law, Daddy, the casino will be in the family anyway,' she pointed out, in case that fact had escaped him.

Lorenzo greeted the revelation with a scowl.

'Look, pet...' He spread his hands. 'You can't blame me for wanting to know more about the man, for not trusting him. A man who just happens to be staying at *our* hotel, who just happened to bump into *you* one day, who just happened to be bidding for the casino, the same as I am...a man who within a matter of days has managed to worm his way into our family and into our home...presumably so that he can delve into our affairs without arousing suspicion. How do we know what the hell he might be up to?'

She tilted her chin. 'Daddy, Mark's a man of integrity, a man of honour and high principles...just as the Danzas are. But he didn't *know* us when he first came here. Can you blame him for wanting to know more about us, for wanting to be sure we weren't, well, like some other wealthy high flyers who aren't particularly...?' She faltered. 'I mean...Mark's not the kind of man who would ever want to get involved with anyone the least bit, well...' This time, as she hesitated, Lorenzo pounced.

'The least bit...what?' His eyes pierced hers.

She shrugged. 'Well...suspect. Not quite...honest.' One look at her father's darkening brow and she added quickly, 'Not that Mark thought——' She broke off impatiently. 'Daddy, he *knows* us now.' But he did still have some lingering reservations about her father, she suspected, sighing at the thought, resulting from some malicious, untrue gossip he'd heard—invented by Hammond, no doubt.

'Well, it's a pity we don't know more about *him*!' Lorenzo fired back.

Verity turned away with a sigh. It was natural, she guessed, trying to see it from her father's point of view, that Lorenzo would have some concern about a man who had proposed to her after knowing her for only a few days. A newcomer, moreover, to their country, who claimed he had no close friends in Australia and no family back home. But Mark wasn't a mere nobody, popping up from nowhere. He was a renowned doctor, with many colleagues in the medical field who would be prepared, she had no doubt, to vouch for him. That must count for something. But her father, she knew, would need more than their word to allay his doubts.

'Daddy, once you get to know Mark,' she appealed to him, 'you'll find that he's everything I've said he is. Please just *try*,' she begged, her eyes huge, intensely blue in her pale face.

'All I'm asking is that you don't rush into anything,' Lorenzo pleaded gruffly in return. 'You've only known him a week. How can you know anyone in only a week—let alone know that you'll want to spend the rest of your life with the man?'

'You told my mother you were going to marry her the first time you met her!' she reminded him, her eyes snapping in triumph. 'And you did marry her—within weeks!'

Lorenzo's great shoulders slumped in a sigh. 'That was different—quite different. I was nearly forty—I wasn't young and impressionable. And your mother and I were from similar backgrounds...we moved in the same circles...we had friends in common, interests in common. She didn't come from a different country, a totally different background, a broken home, a previous marriage... You just tread carefully, my dear. I'm warning you for your own good.'

She drew in a deep breath. 'I know you're only thinking of me, Daddy, and I appreciate that, and love you for it. But marrying Mark is what I want most in all the world, and I would like to have your blessing, Daddy. And I would like to know that you'll give me away at our wedding. Because I do intend to marry

Mark... with or without your blessing. I'll be sad if you refuse to be a part of it... but I'll still go ahead, regardless.'

A heavy silence fell between them. She could feel her father struggling inwardly, knowing that if he refused he could lose her altogether, his precious only daughter.

'You're as stubborn, as headstrong as I am,' he growled at length, his tone weary now, defeated. 'If you're determined to go ahead, then I suppose I'll have to go along with it. But I'm not happy about it, about the way you're rushing into it——'

'Oh, Daddy, *thank you*!' She hurled herself at him, curling her arms around his neck. 'I do love you, Daddy, so much, and I'm so glad you're going to be there for me! I *know* I'm going to be happy with Mark. I love him and need him with all my heart and soul. I've never, never been more sure of anything in my life—and I know Mark feels the same for me!'

'I'd better get to the office.' Lorenzo drew away, catching her hands and holding them for a moment before he let her go. 'Arrange a night for the three of us. Dinner somewhere quiet. An engagement dinner. You can count Gloria out. She's gone away on a two-month cruise.'

Her heart gave a leap of joy at his offer. 'You're not going to try to talk us out of——'

'Do you want an engagement dinner or not?'

'Yes, of course! *Thank* you, Daddy. Can Georgia come too? I want her to be my bridesmaid.'

He scowled. 'If you must. Just arrange it!' He wasn't happy about it, she knew that, but he was prepared to bury his objections for her sake, and go along with what she had decided. Hoping, no doubt, that Johnny, back in America, would manage to dig up some damaging dirt on Mark in time to put a stop to their plans.

Well, she wasn't worried. She wasn't worried in the least.

She met Mark in the Star foyer an hour later, as they'd arranged the previous night. They exchanged a brief kiss, so that anyone watching would have thought they were just good friends, nothing more—although anyone within a couple of metres, seeing Verity's radiant face, would undoubtedly have guessed the truth immediately.

'Daddy's given us his blessing!' she burst out, unable to hold back the good news.

'He approves?' She had surprised him—he had been expecting to hear anything but that.

She side-stepped the question. 'Oh, he'd prefer us to wait... I suppose any parent would. He thinks we're rushing into it, having only known each other a week, and I can see his point, we *are* a——'

She got no further. Mark grasped her arm, his eyes suddenly fierce. 'You're not trying to put the wedding off, are you? You're not saying you won't marry me next month, that you'd rather wait?'

'No, Mark, no...' She looked up at him, saw the strain, the tightness in his face, and thought, He's afraid Daddy's going to talk me out of marrying him altogether. 'I've told Daddy we're getting married next month. He's accepted that. He wants us all to get together—Georgia too—and have a celebration dinner.'

His hands loosened their grip, rubbing gently now where a moment ago they had dug roughly into her skin. 'Well... I must say I'm surprised your father's accepted it so well.' But he was frowning as he said it—he didn't trust her father. She could tell by the iron glint in his eye.

She said quickly, not wanting him to guess what her father had in mind for Johnny over the coming weeks, 'We'd better get going, if we're driving down to Colac to see the marriage celebrant and then on to Tarmaroo to see Georgia.'

As they rode down in the lift to the car park, Mark caught her hand. 'You've switched the ring to your right hand.'

She explained quickly. 'A lot of people know me by sight...reporters, business colleagues of my father, social gossips. If we want to keep our engagement and wedding plans a secret, and out of the papers...don't you think it's a wise thing to do?'

'Ah.' As they stepped out into the underground car park, he drew her arm through his. 'Most girls would want to shout their marriage plans to the world. You're sure you——'

'Quite sure.' She gave a shudder. 'The Press go mad here when anybody in the public eye plans a wedding. They'd have a field day with the daughter of Lorenzo Danza.' She grimaced at the thought.

He swung her round to face him, his eyes burning into hers. 'Verity Danza, you're a rare lady. Completely unspoiled. And level-headed beyond your years. Riches and a high-profile name certainly haven't turned your head!'

'Well, you can thank my father and my aunt Elena for that,' she said, wanting him to know that they were responsible...wanting him to come to like and respect Lorenzo more. Though why he didn't still puzzled her at times. Perhaps, once the casino fight was resolved...

Mark glanced over his shoulder, saw a car nosing into a nearby parking bay, and lightly brushing his lips to her hair, drew away.

'Later,' he said regretfully, and she felt a tiny thrill quivering through her. Once they were out of town, and away from prying eyes, there would be no reason for him not to take her into his arms and kiss her as long and deeply as they both wished.

\* \* \*

It was a glorious day. Not the weather so much—there was a grey blanket of cloud and light drizzle for most of the day—but none of that mattered. To Verity the day was perfect. She was in love, and Mark loved her, and everything was falling beautifully into place.

Georgia's uncle, Wendell Ford, was a stocky, fit-looking man in his early fifties with a competent manner and a gentle sense of humour. With his questions satisfactorily answered—such as could Mark produce proof of his divorce, which was no problem, and show a birth certificate, which was more difficult, but it didn't matter as his passport would suffice—Wendell agreed to marry them in the garden at Tarmaroo. After signing the necessary notice of marriage, tentatively choosing the second Saturday in October, if that date proved agreeable to Georgia, they drove on through drizzling rain to Tarmaroo.

They found Georgia swathed in a Driza-Bone raincoat and a waterproof hat, leading Sultan across the yard to the stables. She was openly delighted with the news, and Verity wondered how she could ever have been jealous of her, even for a moment. Georgia had become like a sister to her over the past months, and if one day Georgia married her brother Johnny she *would* be her sister, and everything, just everything, would be perfect!

Georgia agreed happily to the date they had chosen, offering to help in any way she could. She was overjoyed when Verity asked her to be her bridesmaid.

'Verity, I'd love to. I'd be honoured.'

Verity gave her a hug. 'I'm so glad!'

'You'll have to decide quickly on the guests you want to invite,' Georgia advised. 'It's rather short notice.'

'I know.' Verity squeezed her hand, grateful that the girl sounded more excited than reproving. 'Georgia, Daddy wants to give us an engagement dinner—just the family. And you too, of course. We can make plans then.'

# SHATTERED WEDDING

She asked anxiously, 'Can you come down to town in the next couple of days?'

'I could come down tomorrow, I guess... or even this afternoon. Next week's going to be a bit frantic with the show.'

'Why don't you come back with us after lunch?' Verity asked on an impulse. 'I can ring Daddy and ask him if he'll be free for dinner tonight. We don't want to delay notifying our guests. You can stay in Johnny's apartment overnight.'

Over their lunch Verity suggested that Georgia look for an outfit for the wedding while she was up in town, assuring her that the choice was hers, and that she could select any colour or style that she wished.

'You're only having one bridesmaid?' Georgia asked, catching back the words *this time*. There would have been three if Verity had gone ahead and married Donald—two close friends from her school days, and Donald's sister.

'Just you... yes. My friend Trixie's working overseas now, and Nancy's about to have a baby.' Anyway, she only wanted one bridesmaid this time. The smaller and simpler the ceremony the better.

'And who's going to be your best man, Mark?' Georgia asked, and Verity glanced up at him, curious to hear his answer.

'I could ask my lawyer, Jerry Lydon,' Mark said. 'He's in Sydney at present, handling some business of mine there.'

His business with Jack Hammond, no doubt... Verity heaved a sigh. She had been half hoping that Mark might have decided not to go ahead with it.

'Unless...' Mark was looking at her. 'Unless you'd like to ask your brother Johnny... assuming he's going to be home in time? Jerry could always come as a guest.'

Verity's heart jumped with joy. 'Oh, Mark, do you mean it?' To have Johnny there, supporting Mark...and with Georgia at his side! 'That would be wonderful! I'll ring him tonight,' she cried as Mark smilingly inclined his head. If Johnny knew he was going to be best man at her wedding, surely he would rush through his silly investigations, or brush over them altogether, and come home.

She only hoped, with a tiny shiver, that her father, at their engagement dinner this evening, wouldn't decide to make things difficult, if not intolerable for Mark. She would never forgive him, never, if he drove Mark away from her.

Before dinner, she rang Johnny at Harvard University, holding her breath for fear he might have left there already.

'Johnny Danza speaking.'

'Ah, Johnny, thank goodness! It's Verity.'

'Verry!' Did he sound a trifle guarded? Well, little wonder, in view of the investigating—the *spying*—their father had asked him to do!

Putting that out of her mind, she told Johnny in a rush that she had fallen in love at last, truly in love this time, and in a few quick words told him about Mark and what a wonderful man and a fine doctor he was, and how much he loved *her*, and that they were planning to get married next month at Tarmaroo. And she rushed on before Johnny could speak, telling him that Mark wanted him to be best man at their wedding and that Georgia was going to be her bridesmaid, and begging her brother to be there for her.

When she stopped, a heavy silence followed, and she thought for a moment she had lost the line.

'Johnny? Johnny, are you——?'

'Yes, I'm here. Well, that's great, honey, and I'd be pleased to, but—look, Verry, I don't know when I'll be home...I've some business to deal with after I leave here...it may take a few weeks. Can't you put it off until——?'

'I'm not putting it off,' she cut in sharply. 'And Daddy's already told me what you're up to, Johnny, and I think it stinks! If it gets out that you're nosing around, checking on Mark's background, I'll never speak to you again! And if you're not back here before the second week of October, we'll find ourselves another best man!'

'OK, OK, hold on to your hat! I'm sorry you found out, Verry, but con men do exist, and since you're in such a hurry to tie the knot—Dad tells me you've only known the guy for about a week—surely it's only good sense to make sure there's no...well, impediment. I'll be discretion itself, I promise. And I'll try my best to be back in time.'

'You're sounding more like your father every day,' she said bitterly, and hung up.

How stupid, to have hoped that Johnny would be on her side. How stupid, to have hoped he might only have been humouring their father by agreeing to check up on Mark. Well, he wouldn't find out anything...anything that would shake her love for Mark, at any rate. Who cared what Mark might have done in the past or what his ex-wife said about him or how many other women he'd had before he met her, or anything else for that matter? It would all be a ridiculous waste of time...and it would serve Johnny right if he did miss her wedding!

Lorenzo had booked a private room at one of Melbourne's oldest and finest restaurants for their engagement dinner. On the surface he was civil to Mark, even raising his glass to toast the occasion, but he made no attempt to hold back the questions plaguing him, demanding to know about Mark's family, his medical career, his previous marriage, his reasons for wanting to leave America, until finally, when he started touching on Mark's upbringing in England, Verity called an abrupt halt.

'Daddy, that was a painful time for Mark...and it's very personal.'

'It's all right, Verity.' Mark reached for her hand. 'I don't mind talking about it.' There was a touch of steel in his voice, as if he were challenging Lorenzo to do his worst, to throw anything at him.

'Well, we're not going to talk about it,' Verity said firmly, though the touch of his hand was bringing back memories of things she would much rather be doing than sitting here talking. 'We need to make plans for the wedding. Decide who we intend to invite.' She glanced from her father to Georgia. 'Mark and I want no more than thirty guests—at the most.'

'How many friends and relatives does *he* intend to invite?' Lorenzo growled, without even looking at Mark.

'Only one.' It was Mark who answered, matching Lorenzo's insolence with an edge of scorn. 'My friend and lawyer, Jerry Lydon.'

'You have no other close friends? No relatives?' Frowning, Lorenzo swung slowly round to face him.

'Not here...no. And no one close enough back in America to want to bring them all the way out here.'

'So that gives you and me a free hand, Daddy,' Verity put in swiftly. 'I'll want to invite—say, a dozen friends, including Dee and Tom. You can make up the numbers with any friends and relatives you want.' She drew out a notebook, and started jotting down names, Lorenzo grudgingly adding to the list.

'At such short notice, we'll be lucky if half of them will be able to come,' he grumbled.

Verity brushed that possibility aside. 'As long as my family and the Tarmaroo people are there, who cares?'

'You're prepared to postpone the date if Johnny's not back in time?' Lorenzo asked, eyeing her slyly.

Verity stiffened, her hand tensing under Mark's. So that's what he was hoping! That if Johnny wasn't back, she'd put the wedding off—at the same time giving Johnny a bit longer to produce some damaging facts about Mark that would make her want to call it off for good!

'No, I won't be putting it off,' she said heatedly. 'If Johnny's not back in time, Mark's lawyer will be his best man.' She felt Mark's hand stroking hers, calming her, and she turned to him and smiled.

Georgia intervened hastily. 'Want me to organise the caterers?' she offered. 'And what about the flowers... and a photographer...?'

'We'll be keeping it simple,' Verity stressed. She was thinking of the elaborate plans she had been making with Donald, at his insistence... a full year in advance!

'Of course,' Georgia agreed. 'A simple garden wedding... what could be lovelier? We'll need a marquee,' she said. 'You know how often it rains at Tarmaroo...'

Lorenzo was getting restless, obviously bored with the details. He's going along with the wedding grudgingly, Verity reflected sadly. Hoping the plans will fall through—with or without Johnny's help. But he doesn't want me blaming him when they do.

'Well, ready to go?' Lorenzo finally pushed back his chair.

They all rose and left together, driving back to the Star car park in Lorenzo's big Mercedes. They rode up in the Danza lift together, Verity having invited Mark up to her apartment to help her make a start on the invitations.

But it was really only an excuse to be alone with him... gloriously, wonderfully alone. The invitations didn't get started until much, much later in the evening.

## CHAPTER TEN

SHE could hardly believe it was here at last. Her weddingday... A fine day, too, miraculously—barely a cloud in the sky, and the garden at Tarmaroo looked a picture. The rhododendrons and azaleas and lilacs were in full bloom and a silk-lined marquee graced one end of the lawn.

The past four weeks had flown by. There had been so much to do and think about: house-hunting, preparing for the wedding, selecting a bridal gown, and somehow finding time for work too, Verity having resumed her voluntary work, and Mark having started lecturing at the Children's Hospital.

They had managed to spend most evenings together, occasionally going out, but more often preferring the privacy of Verity's apartment, though Mark, not wanting to alienate Lorenzo further, had always insisted on going back to his hotel room to sleep.

They had drawn even closer in those four weeks, and were now more deeply in love than ever. Verity felt that if anything happened now to spoil their happiness, she would never recover.

There had been no news from Johnny, which was a relief in some ways, but a worry in another, since he still hadn't come home. A little over a week ago she had slipped up to see her father in his apartment before he left for work, to demand that he summon Johnny home. She had found Lorenzo's door partially open, as if he'd been about to leave when something, the phone perhaps, had called him back. She could hear him talking on the phone now. To Johnny, she had quickly realised.

'Well, if it means going to England to find out, then go, damn it! Time's running out. What? OK, son, but keep me informed.'

As he hung up, Verity flew at him in a fury. 'You're so desperate, you're sending Johnny to *England* now? Daddy, this has got to stop—*at once*!' She was so choked up, she could barely speak.

Lorenzo caught her hands, triumph glittering in his eyes. 'Listen to me, pet... Johnny's found evidence that your fiancé's so-called father—Todd Bannister—had only one child—a daughter, who died. *He had no son.* Your Dr Mark Bannister has lied to you, Verity. Why don't you ask him about it?'

The room swayed, and only her father's steely grip saved her from swaying with it. She fought for control, taking a few seconds to pull herself together.

'And admit you've been checking up on him?' she breathed. 'Never!' But instinct told her that it just could be true. It would explain why Mark had never been close to the man he had claimed was his father... and why Todd Bannister, whatever he might have been to Mark, had later turned his back on Mark altogether.

Her mind raced, seeking answers. 'So... Mark must have been born before his mother married Bannister... so what?' she demanded, rallying. 'There are plenty of single mothers in the world. Bannister must have adopted Mark after they got married—and given Mark his name. Mark's never hidden the fact that he and his father—Bannister—were never close, and haven't seen each other since the divorce. No wonder, if Bannister wasn't Mark's real father.'

Lorenzo grunted. 'Maybe. But you can't blame me for wanting to know for sure. If he's lied about that, he could be lying about other things as well.'

'If Todd Bannister adopted Mark,' she shot back, 'then Mark hasn't lied about being his son. Bannister would have been the only father he knew until his mother married again and took him to America. Daddy, I want you to stop this here and now and call Johnny home. I mean it! I don't care about Mark's past and I have no intention of questioning him and admitting that you've been checking up on him. I trust him and I love him and I want you to stop all this *now*!'

Seeing that she meant it, Lorenzo backed down and pulled her into his arms. 'There there, calm down, love, no harm's done—if you're right. With a bit of luck Johnny *will* be home by next week...in time for the wedding.' But his eyes couldn't quite meet hers, and she knew that he was still uneasy, still unhappy about her marrying Mark—for no more reason perhaps than that Mark had opposed his casino bid, and it galled him that his daughter and his rival were rushing headlong into marriage. And no doubt he was still clutching at the hope that Johnny would yet come up with some damaging evidence that would put a stop to the wedding in time.

Well, Johnny hadn't, and the day had arrived, and nothing, *nothing*, Verity thought dreamily, was going to stop them now.

When she emerged from the house on her father's arm, a few paces behind Georgia, an elegant bridesmaid in a burgundy silk suit and matching hat, there were sighs of admiration from the guests on the lawn. Verity was a vision in ivory lace encrusted with tiny pearls, a beautiful old-world gown with a handkerchief hemline and gossamer sleeves threaded with silver and lace. Her black hair was caught back by a cluster of fresh cream roses, its glossy length entwined with white silk ribbon.

She saw Mark standing in front of the garden gazebo with his best man, Jerry Lydon, the two having arrived some time earlier in a hired limousine, after spending the night at a Colac motel. Wendell Ford, formally attired in a grey suit, as befitted his role as celebrant, was standing with them.

Johnny hadn't come. He'd rung the night before to wish her luck and to apologise for not being there... he was caught up in something, he'd told her without explaining, and if she could only wait another day, a few more hours... She had cut him short with a curt laugh and told him coolly that she wasn't going to change her plans simply for him, and that was where they had left it.

Now she was glad that Johnny wasn't there... glad that Mark had a friend of his own by his side, someone he knew supported him, not someone who had been hoping to find some impediment to prevent them marrying. Her eyes sought Mark's as he turned his head, her soft lips curving into a smile. The sight of him, the man she loved, and would always love, brought a lump to her throat. How wonderful he looked, how imposing in his dark suit, how straight and strong and... precious he was to her. If anything had prevented this moment she would have wanted to die.

She felt her father falter at her side, sensed his tension. If only he could be happy for her, she wished with a pang. Surely he must be resigned by now to the fact that Johnny had failed to come up with anything against Mark, and yet... and yet... Her hands trembled on her posy of cream roses. She had never known her father to be so tense, so uptight, his mouth tight, his eyes clouded, almost as if he intended to keep on hoping until the last possible moment.

But at least, she thought in relief, he hadn't backed out of his promise to give her away.

When they reached the gazebo and took their positions on the lawn, Wendell's voice boomed out in the crisp October air, 'Who is giving this woman to be married to this man?'

Verity found she was holding her breath. Her father's hesitation, before he took her hand, was almost imperceptible, but it was enough to send her heart to her mouth. 'I am.'

As Lorenzo stepped back, Verity felt her tense muscles easing. The last hurdle, she thought, her heart soaring, has passed.

Wendell passed her hand to Mark, smiling briefly before he turned to address the small gathering.

'Family and friends of Verity and Mark, we are gathered here today...'

The familiar words, which she and Mark had chosen together in consultation with Wendell, flowed over her. Mark's hand on hers was warm and vibrant, his love, his strength, his happiness seeming to flow from his nerve-ends into hers.

'Mark, will you take Verity to be your lawful wedded wife, will you comfort her, honour and keep her in sickness and in health——'

Verity heard a sharp beeping sound from directly behind, then another beep, abruptly cut off. Her head jerked round, her eyes widening in shocked disbelief when she saw that her father had his mobile phone clamped to his ear. His face was grim, but there was a gleam in his eye. A gleam, she would have sworn, of triumph!

A terrible feeling of foreboding shook through her. The celebrant was still talking, paying no attention...

'—and forsaking all others, keep only unto her, so long as you both——?'

The ceremony had taken on a nightmarish quality, an air of shuddering unreality. When the interruption came, which it did with a suddenness that snapped Wendell

Ford into silence, Verity found, curiously, that she had been expecting it, waiting, paralysed, for the axe to fall.

'*Stop!* Stop the ceremony!'

As he roared the command, Lorenzo thrust his huge bulk between them, tearing Mark from her side, almost knocking him into his best man, Jerry Lydon.

'What the——?' Jerry's protest died on his lips as Lorenzo bellowed over him,

'This man is marrying my daughter under false pretences!'

'Daddy!' Verity croaked, shuddering away from him. 'How—how could you?'

Wendell Ford, looking disconcerted, intervened. 'Excuse us for a moment...please,' he begged the stunned guests, then dropping his voice. 'Perhaps we should go somewhere more——'

'No!' rasped Lorenzo. 'I want everyone to hear this!' He swung round, making sure everyone there could hear. 'This man is not Mark Bannister, as he has claimed. He is Marco Minelli...the son of Bruno Minelli—the lowdown son-of-a-bitch responsible for the death of my wife...Verity's mother!'

# CHAPTER ELEVEN

VERITY gave an agonised cry and slumped against Georgia, her posy of roses slipping from her fingers. Painfully, she forced her gaze to meet Mark's, her heart quailing when she saw, not shock in his face, not denial, but a look of blazing outrage.

'What the hell are you talking about? My father had nothing to do with your wife's death. Your wife died giving birth to Verity!'

Lorenzo pounced. 'So you're not denying that you are Marco Minelli? You're not denying that Bruno Minelli was your father?'

'No, I'm not denying it!' Mark's tone was scathing, his jaw iron-hard, jutting defiance. 'Or regretting it! My only regret is that my father died before his time—a ruined man. Forcing my mother and me—a boy of just seven—to flee our home in Melbourne to start a new life in England!'

Verity gave a whimper, and huddled against Georgia. Mark was admitting that he was the son of her father's oldest and bitterest enemy—an enmity, a hatred, that Lorenzo had always refused to talk about or explain... admitting, too, that he had lived here in Melbourne for the first seven years of his life! Her head spun as she tried to take it all in. And her heart... her heart must surely have broken. But how could she know? She was numb... she couldn't feel a thing.

'My daughter will never marry you now,' Lorenzo vowed, his lip curling with satisfaction as he thrust his face closer to Mark's, his dark eyes jubilant. The scoundrel's humiliation, whether he cared to show it or not, was complete. It had been a close thing though... Johnny's call had come almost too late. But perhaps the impact of it coming out now, at the eleventh hour, and in front of all their friends, made it even more gratifying!

Ignoring Lorenzo, Mark's hard eyes sought Verity's and held them, so that she couldn't pull her stricken gaze away. She thought dazedly: Why isn't Mark showing any sign of shame... any sign of the dreadful humiliation he must be feeling deep inside? Or is he so hard-hearted, so insensitive, that he doesn't feel anything at all?

'I'm *proud* to be Bruno Minelli's son!' Mark said harshly, his compelling gaze still holding hers. 'I only kept the truth from you, Verity, to shield *you*.'

She gave a soft moan, not understanding, wishing she could believe him. She felt torn... hopelessly torn between the man she loved—even this crushing blow hadn't destroyed that, though perhaps she was too numb to realise it yet—and her father, whom she loved too, but whose relentless vow to expose Mark had brought them to this, destroying what should have been the happiest day of her life.

She seized on that, tearing her gaze away from Mark's at last to accuse her father, attack seeming the only resource she had left.

'You chose this moment deliberately, didn't you? You thought that if you humiliated Mark on our wedding-day he'd turn tail and run—or else *I* would. You've been determined all along to break us up. I hope you're satisfied!'

'Pet, I had no idea of the truth until Johnny rang me a few moments ago!' Lorenzo's denial was swift, fervent. 'But I had a gut feeling all along that there must be a good reason the guy was rushing you into marriage. I would have given anything to spare you this... but, dearest, it's better to stop the wedding now than let this bastard have the last laugh on us. If he's anything like his father, he was planning to destroy me—through you!'

With a shocked gasp Verity dragged her gaze back to Mark's. 'Is that true?' she whispered, trembling. 'Have you just been using me? To get close to my father? *Did* you come here to—to destroy my father?'

Her heart seemed to wither and die when he didn't deny it. 'Whatever I had in mind when I first came here, Verity, I rejected it when I fell in love with you.' But there was no warmth, no gentleness in his tone. His voice was as cold, as hard as stone.

With a cry, she crushed her fist to her lips, muffling her agony.

Jerry Lydon, with his capable lawyer's training, swiftly stepped in, beckoning to the hovering waiters.

'Take the guests to the marquee and serve them drinks...now!' he commanded, and, as they jumped to obey, Wendell Ford touched Lorenzo's arm.

'Let's thrash it out in the house. This isn't the place...'

'Right,' Lorenzo grated, and Mark gave a stony nod. As the celebrant ushered the family away, Jerry Lydon appealed to the guests.

'The family needs to talk in private. We regret that this has happened, but please...don't waste all that food and drink!'

'Help Jerry look after the guests, Georgia,' Verity called numbly over her shoulder as she accepted Wendell's supporting arm.

Once inside, she sank wearily into an armchair while Wendell hovered between Lorenzo and Mark, as if afraid the two might come to blows. Neither Lorenzo nor Mark would sit down, both electing to stand and face each other belligerently, as if to sit down might have given the other an advantage.

Verity's choked voice broke the terrible silence. 'I'll never forgive you for this, Daddy...never! You're—

you're trying to ruin my life! You've already ruined m-my wedding-day!'

Lorenzo swung round to face her. 'Pet, I only spoke up to *protect* you.'

'No, you didn't!' Angry tears glistened on her lashes. 'You've done this out of vengeance... to hit back at the Minelli family—a family you've always hated, for some hidden reason of your own. I don't *care*. And don't tell me you were thinking of *me*,' she warned, her voice trembling. 'All you've succeeded in doing is to *hurt* me. I *love* Mark, Daddy. I don't care what his father did...it's nothing to do with Mark and me!'

Lorenzo looked down at her, his eyes flaring in faint surprise, as if he had expected her to be crushed, humiliated, by Mark's deception. 'You don't care that this man has lied to you...deceived you...used a false name to insinuate himself into your confidence, into our lives, so that he could spy on us, hurt us...me in particular? You haven't forgotten that underhand casino bid of his?' he reminded her with a sneer. 'Lord knows what else he had in mind, once he was married to you!'

As Verity sagged in her chair, Lorenzo turned sharply, blazing at Mark, 'Now perhaps you'd like to tell us precisely what you *did* have in mind when you came to Melbourne—came *back* to Melbourne after all these years—and just why you chose to insinuate yourself into our lives!'

Mark faced him unflinchingly, his eyes icy with contempt. 'A year ago I didn't know the Danza family existed. At that time I was simply planning to revisit the place where I was born... and to attend a medical congress in Melbourne. But when my mother heard about my plans, she flew into a panic. She made me swear not to mention a word to anyone out here who my real father had been, not even to mention the Minelli name. It could be dangerous, she said... for me. It was only then, for the first time, that she revealed the truth about what you, Lorenzo Danza, had done to my father.'

Mark's voice was harsh, gratingly hostile. 'Once I knew the full ugly story, my prime reason for coming to Melbourne,' his eyes raked Lorenzo's face with bitter contempt, 'was to damage and if possible ruin *you*...the way you ruined my father!'

As shock slapped through Verity—none of this could be true, it couldn't!—she saw her father move threateningly towards Mark, his face suffused with savage fury.

As Wendell Ford thrust his stout body between them, Lorenzo roared over him, 'You were planning to marry my daughter to hit back at *me*?'

Verity held her breath. Why, she wondered dimly, wasn't her father denying that he had ruined Mark's father? And why didn't he seem surprised that Mark would want to hit back at him?

'Your daughter has nothing to do with this!' Mark's tone was withering. 'I'm in love with Verity. It's because of her that I didn't go through with it!'

Lorenzo rasped, 'You mean you love what she would have handed you on a platter if you'd married her!'

'I don't need anything from you!' Mark denied with biting scorn. 'I have all I want.' His eyes scorched into Verity's. 'If she'll still have me after this!' He swung back to face Lorenzo, his eyes turning to silver shards of ice. 'You destroyed my father, Lorenzo Danza. Coldly, deliberately, without pity. You left him and my mother and me with nothing. Disgraced—and penniless! The strain of it killed my father. He died of a massive heart attack—at the age of forty-three. I lay his death at your door!'

Lorenzo's head jerked back, his eyes burning with a strange fire. 'He got what he deserved!'

Verity gave a muffled groan. Was he admitting, she thought in strangled horror, that he had deliberately, cold-bloodedly, ruined Mark's father, and caused his death?

'You and your mother did all right,' Lorenzo rasped at Mark. 'You still had friends...relatives back in Italy.'

'My mother was English, not Italian,' Mark ground back. 'She didn't want her husband's family in Italy claiming me—taking me away from her. As for friends...they vanished when they knew we were broke. My mother's family back in England paid for us to go to England. She was terrified that you'd come after *her* if we stayed here in Australia. It was only after she remarried and changed her name, she told me, that she started to feel safe.'

Lorenzo gave a snort. 'Your mother had nothing to fear from me.'

'Didn't she? You'd destroyed my father because he knew something about you—something you didn't want to come out. If you'd thought that *she* knew too...that my father might have told *her* what he knew... Do you blame her for being afraid? And for warning me to be wary of Lorenzo Danza when she knew I was planning to come back to Melbourne?'

'Daddy...' With a whimper, Verity managed to find her voice, a thin, pathetic little sound. 'Is all this true? Did you d-deliberately ruin Mark's father? And what does Mark mean—that it was because of something his father knew about you?' she added in a tense whisper.

Lorenzo's lip curled in disgust. 'Bruno Minelli knew nothing—because there *was* nothing to know. His wife must have *assumed* he had something on me, *assumed* that was the reason I'd ruined her husband. Because Minelli would never have had the guts to tell her the truth—the real reason I ruined him. I ruined him because of what he did to my family!'

'D-Daddy, w-what are you saying?' Verity felt a terrible fear clutching at her heart. It wasn't so much the fear of hearing what her father had to say... it was more the fear of losing Mark. Already she could feel him slipping away from her, second by second. Without even realising it, she had risen to her feet, and was standing close to him, without actually touching him, sensing that any second from now he might need her support—though whether he'd accept it...

Mark showed no sign that she was even there. His eyes, burning with scorn, were fixed to Lorenzo's face. 'Why would my father want to hurt your family?' he rasped.

Lorenzo gave a scowl. 'Minelli always had a grudge against me... ever since the day I pulled out of a development project he'd talked me into up in Queensland.'

'You're talking about my father's resort hotel up on the Gold Coast,' Mark said flatly, a savage glint in his eyes. 'My mother told me about that. How my father had asked you to be his partner in the venture. He would provide the basic investment capital if you would provide the management and development expertise and a limited amount of additional capital. You agreed.'

'Reluctantly,' Lorenzo conceded, his tone still harsh. 'I was uncertain about the site he'd chosen, and about *him*. His reputation was... questionable. I knew he'd been involved in some dubious get-rich-quick schemes in the past.'

'Imprudent schemes, perhaps, but perfectly legal—at the time,' Mark said coldly. 'My mother was aware of them. She also knew they were behind him—and regretted—when he married her, and long before I came along.'

'So Minelli tried to convince me.' There was a sneer in Lorenzo's voice. 'He wanted that partnership badly. He wanted to show the business world he'd become respectable, worthy of their trust. People knew I wouldn't do business with anyone who wasn't honest and beyond reproach.'

'Like yourself?' Mark's tone was icy with scorn.

Lorenzo scowled. 'Yes, like myself!' he snapped. 'But even I have made mistakes... and agreeing to go into that project with your father was one of them. Fool that I was, I let him go ahead and publicise the project. There was a big splash about it in the papers. The final documents were ready to be signed when my lawyers—I'd had them checking Minelli out, just to make sure he was as clean as he swore he was—found out that he'd been involved in a big drug deal only months before. An Italian friend of his had organised the operation, and Minelli had financed it. Narcotics!' His lip curled in revulsion.

As Verity gave a shocked gasp, Mark cut in harshly, 'My father was totally unaware of that drug operation—until it was all over! He was innocent—my mother told me all about it. My father was *used*. That Italian so-called *friend* of his had pleaded with my father to give him a loan... a large loan. He swore it was to pay off his business debts. He offered my father high interest on the loan. For old times' sake—they *had* been friends once, living in the same street—my father agreed. OK, it was naïve of him, but that was my father all over. He'd do anything for a friend.'

'That money was used to buy narcotics!' Lorenzo spat out.

'My father found that out... too late, unfortunately for him.' Mark eyed Lorenzo coldly. 'He'd genuinely believed that the money was going to be used to pay back this guy's massive debt. He made a mistake... a big one. But my father was no criminal. He despised drugs and everything to do with them. He lost a lot of money over it—he never got it back—but he kept quiet about it. He didn't want his reputation tarnished, to have people believe that he *had* been involved. And then you...' Mark's eyes raked over Lorenzo with withering contempt. 'Without warning, you pulled out of the partnership. Without a word of explanation, without even giving my father a chance to explain.'

Lorenzo thrust out his jaw. 'If I'd given him the chance to explain, how could I have been sure he was telling the truth and not just making excuses, covering up? I had no intention of having dealings with a man I couldn't be sure of, and didn't trust. I couldn't afford to take the risk. My reputation was too valuable to me. I'd never liked the site he'd chosen anyway—there were too many resorts along the Gold Coast already. I found a better location further north, up on the Sunshine Coast, and built a bigger and better resort there—on my own. It's done well.'

'While my father's failed!' Mark clenched his fists, fighting back his anger. 'When you backed out of that joint venture, my father was forced to struggle on by himself, against impossible odds. He'd already lost money on that other rotten business, and now he lost a lot more. He lacked the expertise you would have provided. And the personal damage it did to his reputation—the rumours when you backed out—damaged him even further. People avoided his resort. It was no wonder it failed.'

'It was Minelli's decision to go ahead...on his own.' Lorenzo's voice held no pity. 'He could have backed out...or found another partner. He chose not to.' His face tightened. 'In his own typical way, he blamed me when it didn't do well and he lost money on it. He couldn't accept it, take any of the blame himself...he had to hit back at *me*.' A muscle jumped at his temple. 'And he chose the lowest, most diabolical way!'

A deathly hush fell.

'I think you'd better explain what you mean,' Mark said, his eyes narrowed to silvery slits, his tone laced with scorn.

Lorenzo's face twitched. He was looking at Verity now, not at Mark, his dark eyes wavering, and strangely haunted. 'I've never spoken about it before... I didn't want to distress *you*, pet,' he said, and for the first time his voice had lost its harsh edge.

Her eyes widened, a shiver feathering down her spine. 'Tell me, Daddy. There have been too many secrets for far too long. Tell me!'

'Yes...you're right.' Lorenzo heaved a sigh. 'No more secrets.' He threw a virulent look in Mark's direction. When he went on, his voice was cold, in control again. 'Bruno Minelli chose a revenge so cruelly vicious that it shocked my wife into an early labour—a difficult labour, five weeks too early. Complications set in. She died giving birth to Verity.' His black eyes bored accusingly into Mark's stony face. 'Verity never knew her mother because of Bruno Minelli—because of your father!'

Shock held them immobile for a few seconds. Verity could feel Mark's tension, even though she still wasn't touching him. Wendell Ford stood grimly silent, a shadowy presence behind.

Mark was the one who spoke first, breaking the agonising silence.

'Tell me what my father did!' he rasped. 'What was this vicious revenge you believe he took?'

Lorenzo turned to him, his face tight, jaw clenched, but his eyes were unseeing, still haunted, as if he had drifted back into the past.

'My wife's pregnancy was going well,' he began tonelessly. 'Then one night she had a phone call from a stranger. I was away at the time, negotiating some business in Sydney. It meant flying up there often, though

I never spent more than one or two nights away from home at a time, and I kept in constant contact.'

His face twitched as he paused to draw breath. 'The stranger on the line told my wife I was playing around. He'd seen me with this beautiful young woman in Sydney, numerous times, and again in Brisbane, and everybody, he said, knew about it and was talking about it. He told my wife I was planning to divorce her as soon as the baby was born. As you can imagine, my wife was devastated.'

Verity choked back a gasp. 'You mean—that's what triggered my mother's early labour? The shock of hearing those lies?'

Lorenzo held up his hand. 'There's more. On the same night my wife received that phone call, I received a phone call myself. From a man who told me that the child my wife was expecting wasn't mine. He said she'd had a short-lived affair with our gardener at Tarmaroo while I was away overseas months earlier. The gardener had since left Melbourne, and disappeared. She'd *paid* him to disappear, the voice told me.'

'Oh, Daddy! You didn't *believe* him? An anonymous caller!'

A spasm crossed Lorenzo's face. 'I didn't know what to believe. I loved her so much—she was so beautiful, so precious to me, and there were times when I *was* jealous of other men. I was constantly afraid of losing her. I...saw red. I flew straight home to confront her. I had to know!'

In the pause that followed, nobody spoke. Mark's body seemed carved from stone. Verity could barely breathe. Wendell stood behind, his broad hands clenched together, looking ready to intervene if blows ensued.

'The moment I saw her face,' Lorenzo went on heavily, 'I thought—it's true! The way she greeted me...she wasn't pleased to see me. She shrank from me, as if she saw in my face that I knew. She must have been thinking I'd come home to tell her about my so-called other woman! The strain of it—the distress—caused her labour to start, and I had to rush her to the hospital.' His face squeezed with anguish.

'Oh Daddy!' Verity's hand fluttered towards him. 'How terrible! But did you have a chance to reassure her before——?'

'Thank God—yes. I had time during that terrible labour to tell her I didn't care if the baby wasn't mine, *she* was all I cared about. She was horrified, demanding to know where I'd got such a crazy idea. When I told her, she told me about the phone call *she* had received... but it was too late!' His voice broke, and he turned away, as if he couldn't bear the sight of Mark anywhere near him.

Verity touched her father's arm. 'Daddy...' She forced out the question. 'What—what makes you think it was Mark's father who...?'

Lorenzo turned and looked down at her. His voice harsh again, he said, 'I found out the day after your mother's death notice appeared in the paper. The man his father had hired to do his dirty work for him, to make those calls, rang me—he must have got cold feet, or a twinge of conscience, I don't know—and told me he'd been paid to make those calls. I demanded to know by whom, but he refused to tell me until I agreed to send him a sum of money and give him twenty-four hours to get out of town. I agreed—and he told me it was Bruno Minelli. This man's father!' he spat out, eyeing Mark with loathing.

Verity swung round to catch Mark's arm. But he looked more outraged than in need of support, his body taut, rock-like, sending out waves of rejection, his arms clenched at his sides, his jaw jutting in arrogant defiance. Stifling a groan, she let her hand flutter away.

Was he even rejecting *her*? And even if he weren't, how could they ever have a future together with all this between them?

'What was the man's name?' Mark rapped at Lorenzo. 'The man who rang you? The man who put the blame on my father!'

Lorenzo's lip curled. 'He called himself Lennie Rocket. That's all I knew about him. He left town, just as he said he would. He would hardly have wanted your father catching up with him!'

'Lennie Rocket!' Mark gave a snort of disgust. '*He* was the one who told those lies, who put the blame on my father? That slimy little creep? And you *believed* him?' he scoffed.

'So he *was* a friend of your family!' Lorenzo rasped in triumph. 'How else would you have heard of him?'

'The little weasel was no friend of my family's—far from it! But my mother knew about him, and told me about him. About how he used to work for *you*... as your chauffeur. Only he called himself Larry Morgan then!' Now it was Mark's turn to look triumphant, as Lorenzo stirred uneasily.

'You mean Lennie Rocket was *Larry Morgan*... the man I once dismissed for stealing confidential papers from me? Who stole from me with the intention of selling to the highest bidder!'

'So that was why you dismissed him. My mother didn't know the reason... she only knew that Larry Morgan—or Lennie Rocket, as he'd decided to call himself—held a grudge against you because of it. Some time after you gave him the sack, the little weasel came to my father—knowing my father had also had a falling out with you. Rocket proposed they join forces to hit back at you in some way... some *personal* way. He said *he'd* do whatever had to be done if my father would pay him enough so that he could afford to skip town afterwards. My father was disgusted. He kicked Rocket out. He would have nothing to do with it. The little rat must have gone ahead and made those slimy calls anyway, on his own, and then extracted payment from *you*. If my father had anything to blame himself for,' Mark added slowly, his voice still hard, 'it was in not warning you to watch out for Rocket. Not that you and he were exactly on speaking terms!'

Lorenzo's breath hissed through his teeth. 'Rocket swore to me that it was Bruno Minelli's idea to hit back at me. Swore Bruno had paid him to do it.'

'Would you have believed him if you'd known he was Larry Morgan, the chauffeur you'd dismissed for stealing from you?' Mark demanded. 'A thief who would do anything for money? And obviously, anything, short of physical violence, for revenge!'

A taut silence fell. It was Lorenzo who finally broke it. 'So it was Larry Morgan, not Bruno Minelli, who was responsible for my wife's death.' He sounded drained now, exhausted, his great shoulders slumping. '*He* was the one who wrecked my life, whose cruelty lost me the only woman I've ever loved—will ever love—and denied my daughter and son a mother. And the bastard got away with it! He put the blame on Bruno Minelli so that I wouldn't come after *him*. And to think I actually paid the swine! Hell, I'd like to——'

'Daddy!' Verity cried in alarm. 'Now don't *you* start thinking of revenge,' she pleaded. 'It all happened a long time ago, and even if Mark's father *had* been involved Mark himself would have been completely blameless. You could never have held it against *him*.'

Lorenzo bowed his head, suddenly a defeated old man. 'You don't understand,' he said brokenly. 'I've made a ghastly mistake, a mistake I can never make up for. I ruined Bruno. I blamed him for your mother's death. I ruined him...coldly and methodically, thinking he was getting what he deserved. An innocent man!'

'Mr Danza...' Mark's voice, for the first time, had lost its harshness.

But Lorenzo held up his hand, eyeing Mark bleakly from under his heavy brows. 'You might as well know it all, know *how* I ruined your father. It wasn't too difficult,' he said, self-recrimination heavy in his voice. 'Bruno was already in financial difficulties. I knew he was planning to tender for a big new project in Sydney—one he was desperate to win. So I put in a bid myself, a deliberately low bid, anonymously leaking the low quote so that Bruno would find out. I knew he'd go lower, try anything to defeat my bid. I had already foreseen that there was a credit squeeze coming—I knew things would tighten up. I let Bruno win the bid, squeezing his resources so badly that he had to borrow heavily to finance it—as I'd known he would. Then the credit squeeze hit, and he was finished. Ruined. The strain of it...' He gave a deep shudder.

'Brought on his fatal heart attack,' Mark finished tonelessly. He sucked in his breath. 'My mother always believed that you ruined my father because you were afraid he was about to expose you for something he'd found out about you...something shady that *you* had been involved in.'

Verity touched his arm. 'And that was why you opposed Daddy's casino bid...you wanted to hit back at *him*,' she whispered. 'And it's why you've always doubted Daddy's honesty, his integrity...'

Mark bent his head, his eyes seeking hers, holding her gaze. 'Yes,' he said. 'When I first came here I was hoping to find out what your father was hiding, and use it to hurt *him*—even ruin him if I could, the way he'd ruined my father.'

As Verity's lips parted, he added swiftly, tenderness in his voice now. 'But you...you were a complication I hadn't expected, or allowed for. As I got to know you,

you convinced me that you knew nothing about any shady dealings of your father's. In your eyes your father was squeaky-clean, beyond reproach. I still didn't believe it, but obviously *you* did... and because I was in love with you by then, and didn't want to lose you, I buried all thought of revenge... I only wanted *you*.'

'And that was why you wanted to rush her into marrying you,' Lorenzo spoke up, an accusing note now in his voice. 'You wanted her safely married to you before she found out who you really were!'

Mark turned slowly, not denying it. 'I wanted her safely married to me—yes—but it was so that I could give her my protection, my love, when the truth about you came out... so that I could help her through it. You see, Mr Danza, I intended to confront you after the wedding... to have it out with you, and demand an admission that you had ruined my father—and an explanation. I was hoping to bring you to your knees, and when I had I was prepared to put it all behind me, for Verity's sake. But I see now that your motives were...' He paused, a glint of pity in his eyes now as he looked at Lorenzo. 'Rather different from what I expected. I wronged you in thinking that you had something criminal to hide, that it was fear of discovery that prompted you to destroy my father. You believed my father was responsible for your wife's death, that he had destroyed your life...'

'I'll never forgive myself for believing that swine Larry Morgan... or Rocket or whatever he called himself.' Lorenzo clenched his great fists. He added with a heavy sigh, 'I can't make amends for that... but there is one thing I can do. I can withdraw from the casino race.'

'No!' Mark curtly dismissed the offer. 'I only went into it to hurt *you*. Now that I know the full story— know your motivation for ruining my father—winning the casino bid over you no longer matters to me. I have other priorities now.' He was looking at Verity as he spoke. 'The new company I formed for the express purpose of supporting Jack Hammond's bid for the casino... I intend to hand it over to you, Mr Danza. The company will be yours to do whatever you like with. You can remain in the consortium, joining forces with Hammond to secure the casino bid, or you can sever all connection with him and go it alone. You'd be sure of winning, either way.'

Lorenzo's jaw dropped. 'That is extremely generous of you. But,' he sighed, looking sadly down at his misty-eyed daughter, 'it doesn't really change anything. After all this, my dear, you must see that a marriage between a Danza and a Minelli is impossible.'

'I was a Minelli a long time ago,' Mark cut in. 'I'm Mark Bannister now, and have been ever since my mother married again when I was eight years old and my stepfather officially adopted me.'

Lorenzo gave him a long considering look. 'But you must see that the past would always be there between our families.' He spread his hands. 'And especially between you and Verity. You must hate me,' he said, shaking his head at Mark. 'And Verity...she's *my* daughter!'

'I don't hate you, Mr Danza. I can even, in a way, understand your motives. If I had been in your position...believed what you believed... I might have been driven to do the same.'

Lorenzo's eyes flickered. 'That's——'

'Daddy, I *love* Mark!' Verity moved suddenly, catching Mark's arm, a determined gleam in her eyes. 'I love him the way you loved my mother. Can't you understand? *Nothing* will stop me marrying him! Nothing will keep me from him!'

Lorenzo turned to her, his dark eyes smouldering under his thick brows. 'Verity, my dear, you need time—

you both do—to let all this sink in. To consider the...ramifications. With all the old hatred between our families, are you sure a marriage between you could work? Dearest, all I'm asking is that you don't rush into a decision now. Give yourself some time—a week at least—to think things over, to work out what is best— for both of you. For all of us. You're in no fit emotional state right now... I'm sure Mark will agree with me.' It was the first time he had called Mark by his given name. 'I'm sure he'll need time himself to think about all this, to decide what's... best.'

'Your father is talking sense, Verity,' Mark agreed quietly, and when she looked up at him the eyes that met hers were shuttered, unreadable. Was he deliberately backing away, deliberately trying to push her out of his life?

She panicked. 'You're saying—you don't love me any more?' She caught her breath, struck by an even greater fear. 'You n-never loved me? You *were* only marrying me to—to strike back at my father?' She leapt back away from him as if stung.

A spasm crossed Mark's face. 'If you can believe that, Verity, then there's no point thinking things over even for a day.'

Wendell Ford intervened, touching Lorenzo's arm. 'I think we should go out and speak to your guests. They deserve an explanation, though just what...'

'You're right.' Lorenzo heaved a sigh. 'I'll speak to them. I'll tell them I was grossly mistaken about Bruno Minelli—that there was a misunderstanding and they can forget about the comments I made. I'll tell them that Mark was legally adopted at an early age by an Englishman called Bannister and hasn't been Marco Minelli since he was eight years old. That's all they need to know.'

Verity's eyes were moist as Lorenzo, straightening his shoulders, strode from the room. As Wendell Ford moved to follow him she cried, 'Wait, Wendell...please!' and the celebrant paused, turning to face her.

She flew across the room, caught his arm, and whispered a few words in his ear. In response, he patted her arm, shot Mark a rallying smile, and stepped from the room.

She turned and looked at Mark. For a few seconds they faced each other across the room, she pale-faced and exquisitely beautiful in her lace wedding-gown, he standing motionless, his arms hanging at his sides, only the tenseness in his hands giving him away.

After what seemed an endless moment his lips moved. 'Your father is right, Verity. You need time to think about all this...there's no rush any longer,' he said, a touch of irony in his voice. 'You know it all now. You need time to consider whether you could live with the fact that I came out here to hurt your family...or if you want your father reminded, each time he sees me, of what he did to my father, my family...' He shook his head. 'Won't it hurt you, Verity, to see your father in pain because of my constant presence?' he asked gently. 'Are either of you ever likely to forget what I came down here to do?'

'You'd be marrying *me*, Mark, not my father!' she cried in a strangled voice, desperation clutching at her throat.

'Verity, you're very close to your father. You spend——'

'He has Gloria...and his work...and Johnny will be home soon! My father's a strong man, Mark. He'll get over it. He likes you already, I know he does, and he respects you, and understands why you wanted to hurt him. He's out there now speaking up for you, taking all the blame on himself. But it wouldn't matter anyway, because it's only you and me who matter. It's *you* I want, Mark. Only you!'

Mark smiled, a rueful little smile. 'You might feel that way now. But are you sure you'll still feel the same way in a week's time, a month, a year? Can you be sure you'll ever be able to forget what I came here to do to your family?'

'Mark, I understand why you wanted revenge... I do! That's all behind us now...forever. I love you, and I always will. If you love me...'

He gave a groan. 'If I love you!' He took an agonised step towards her, then stopped, shaking his head. 'You still doubt it, don't you?'

She gave a cry of denial and came to life, running to him, clutching at his arms. 'Oh, Mark, I don't doubt it, I know that you love me, and I love *you* so much that I would follow you anywhere...to America, to England, to *Timbuctoo* if necessary—even if it meant never seeing my family again! And I *am* going to marry you, Mark. And I don't intend to wait, not for a week, not for a day, not for an *hour*. I'm going to marry you here, today...*now*!'

'You mean——'

'I mean *now*, Mark.'

# EPILOGUE

THE bride was smiling radiantly as she walked out of the house for the second time on Lorenzo's arm, rejoicing in the knowledge that this time she had her father's willing support. If he still had reservations about holding the wedding now, today, he showed no sign of it, his dark eyes smiling down at her, his arm gently squeezing hers, showing no sign of the tension he had been under the previous time.

Convinced finally of their love for each other, their lifelong commitment to each other, Lorenzo had bowed to their decision to go ahead with the ceremony, raising no further arguments, his own memories of his deep love for Verity's mother helping to break down his defences.

All the guests were there waiting for them, Wendell Ford, at Verity's urging, having spoken to them earlier, asking them to stay, and not one of them had left.

Mark was standing in front of the gazebo, his head half turned, his gaze seeking hers, the warmth of his love blazing from his eyes.

She smiled back, knowing that they had chosen the right moment, knowing that everything was all right now, that nothing was going to happen this time to spoil it.

And nothing did. This time the ceremony went ahead without a breath of disruption, with no hostility, no tension, nothing to destroy the most magical, meaningful day of their lives. The traumas of earlier, the fact that the air had been cleared at last, seemed only to intensify their happiness, to add to their confidence in the future.

And afterwards, under the big marquee, their friends and relatives crowded round them, showering them with love and support. The only one missing was Johnny, and Verity could hardly wait for him to come home and hear the full story, for Mark and Johnny to become friends—and, hopefully, to see Johnny and Georgia find the same happiness together that she knew she was going to have with Mark.

That evening, as she lay in Mark's arms in the family's beach house at Apollo Bay, where they had driven after the wedding festivities were over and the guests had all left, she whispered dreamily, to the sound of the waves breaking on the shore outside their window,

'Mark, darling... let's forget about flying to Hawaii tomorrow and go to that house auction in town. You know, that lovely house in Toorak we looked at the other day...the one with the big comfortable living-rooms and all those bedrooms and that huge garden. It would make a wonderful family home, don't you think? And it's so close to town, to our work...'

'Mmm...and deliciously private.' Mark nibbled at her ear. 'Sounds good to me.'

'You mean...we can? You don't mind putting off Hawaii?' She curled her arms around his neck. 'We can go later... once we know that we'll have a home to come back to, a place of our very own to move into...'

'Who needs Hawaii?' Mark's voice was muffled as he buried his face in the silky mass of her hair. 'We have it all here anyway... golden beaches, the sea, the sun... and each other. What else do we need?'

'Nothing,' she said, and added, smiling contentedly up at him. 'Nothing...well, not for at least nine months!'

# SUMMER SPECIAL!

**Four exciting new Romances for the price of three**

Each Romance features British heroines and their encounters with dark and desirable Mediterranean men. *Plus, a free Elmlea recipe booklet inside every pack.*

So sit back and enjoy your sumptuous summer reading pack and indulge yourself with the free Elmlea recipe ideas.

Available July 1994                    Price £5.70

## MILLS & BOON

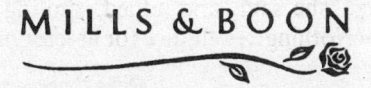

*Available from WH Smith, John Menzies, Volume One, Forbuoys, Martins, Woolworths, Tesco, Asda, Safeway and other paperback stockists. Also available from Mills & Boon Reader Service, FREEPOST, PO Box 236, Croydon, Surrey CR9 9EL. (UK Postage & Packing free)*

# Next Month's Romances

Each month you can choose from a wide variety of romance with Mills & Boon. Below are the new titles to look out for next month, why not ask either Mills & Boon Reader Service or your Newsagent to reserve you a copy of the titles you want to buy – just tick the titles you would like and either post to Reader Service or take it to any Newsagent and ask them to order your books.

| *Please save me the following titles:* | Please tick | ✓ |
|---|---|---|
| **THE SULTAN'S FAVOURITE** | Helen Brooks | |
| **INFAMOUS BARGAIN** | Daphne Clair | |
| **A TRUSTING HEART** | Helena Dawson | |
| **MISSISSIPPI MOONLIGHT** | Angela Devine | |
| **TIGER EYES** | Robyn Donald | |
| **COVER STORY** | Jane Donnelly | |
| **LEAP OF FAITH** | Rachel Elliot | |
| **EVIDENCE OF SIN** | Catherine George | |
| **THE DAMARIS WOMAN** | Grace Green | |
| **LORD OF THE MANOR** | Stephanie Howard | |
| **INHERITANCE** | Shirley Kemp | |
| **PASSION'S PREY** | Rebecca King | |
| **DYING FOR YOU** | Charlotte Lamb | |
| **NORAH** | Debbie Macomber | |
| **PASSION BECOMES YOU** | Michelle Reid | |
| **SHADOW PLAY** | Sally Wentworth | |

If you would like to order these books in addition to your regular subscription from Mills & Boon Reader Service please send £1.90 per title to: Mills & Boon Reader Service, Freepost, P.O. Box 236, Croydon, Surrey, CR9 9EL, quote your Subscriber No:................................. (if applicable) and complete the name and address details below. Alternatively, these books are available from many local Newsagents including W H Smith, J Menzies, Martins and other paperback stockists from 12 August 1994.

Name:..................................................................................
Address:...............................................................................
....................................................Post Code:........................

**To Retailer:** If you would like to stock M&B books please contact your regular book/magazine wholesaler for details.

You may be mailed with offers from other reputable companies as a result of this application.
If you would rather not take advantage of these opportunities please tick box. ☐

# HEARTS OF FIRE

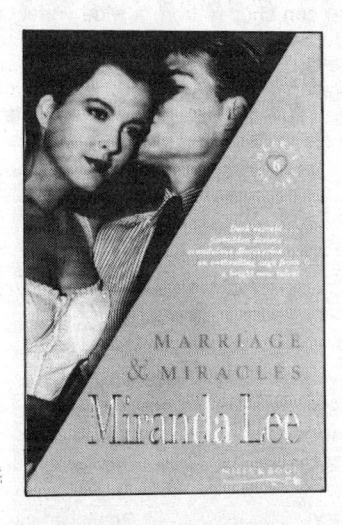

Gemma's marriage to Nathan is in tatters, but she is sure she can win him back if only she can teach him the difference between lust and love...

She knows she's asking for a miracle, but miracles can happen, can't they?

**The answer is in Book 6...**

**MARRIAGE & MIRACLES
by Miranda Lee**

**The final novel in the compelling HEARTS OF FIRE saga.**

Available from August 1994                    Priced: £2.50

## MILLS & BOON

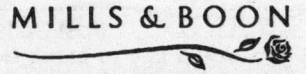

*Available from WH Smith, John Menzies, Volume One, Forbuoys, Martins, Woolworths, Tesco, Asda, Safeway and other paperback stockists.
Also available from Mills & Boon Reader Service, FREEPOST, PO Box 236, Croydon, Surrey CR9 9EL (UK Postage & Packing free).*

# *Full of Eastern Passion...*

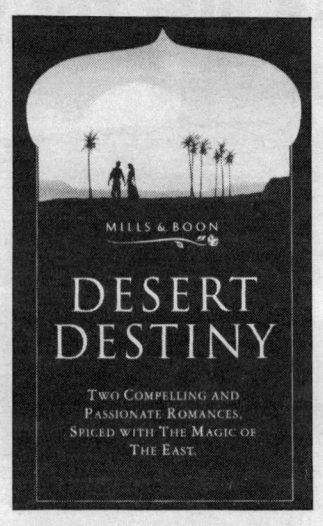

**MILLS & BOON**

## DESERT DESTINY

TWO COMPELLING AND
PASSIONATE ROMANCES,
SPICED WITH THE MAGIC OF
THE EAST.

Savour the romance of the East this summer with
our two full-length compelling Romances,
wrapped together in one exciting volume.

**AVAILABLE FROM 29 JULY 1994   PRICED £3.99**

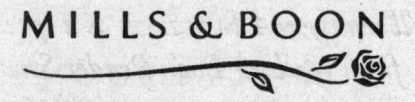

# MILLS & BOON

*Available from WH Smith, John Menzies, Volume One, Forbuoys, Martins,
Woolworths, Tesco, Asda, Safeway and other paperback stockists.
Also available from Mills & Boon Reader Service, FREEPOST,
PO Box 236, Croydon, Surrey CR9 9EL. (UK Postage & Packing free)*

# 4 FREE
## Romances and 2 FREE gifts just for you!

*You can enjoy all the heartwarming emotion of true love for FREE! Discover the heartbreak and happiness, the emotion and the tenderness of the modern relationships in Mills & Boon Romances.*

*We'll send you 4 Romances as a special offer from Mills & Boon Reader Service, along with the opportunity to have 6 captivating new Romances delivered to your door each month.*

**Claim your FREE books and gifts overleaf...**

# An irresistible offer from Mills & Boon

Become a regular reader of Romances with Mills & Boon Reader Service and we'll welcome you with 4 books, a CUDDLY TEDDY and a special MYSTERY GIFT all absolutely FREE.

And then look forward to receiving 6 brand new Romances each month, delivered to your door hot off the presses, postage and packing FREE! Plus our free Newsletter featuring author news, competitions, special offers and much more.

This invitation comes with no strings attached. You may cancel or suspend your subscription at any time, and still keep your free books and gifts.

It's so easy. Send no money now. Simply fill in the coupon below and post it to -
Reader Service, FREEPOST, PO Box 236, Croydon, Surrey CR9 9EL.

---

**NO STAMP REQUIRED**

## Free Books Coupon

**Yes!** Please rush me 4 FREE Romances and 2 FREE gifts! Please also reserve me a Reader Service subscription. If I decide to subscribe I can look forward to receiving 6 brand new Romances for just £11.40 each month, postage and packing FREE. If I decide not to subscribe I shall write to you within 10 days - I can keep the free books and gifts whatever I choose. I may cancel or suspend my subscription at any time. I am over 18 years of age.

Ms/Mrs/Miss/Mr _____ EP71R

Address _____

_____

Postcode _____ Signature _____

Offers closes 31st October 1994. The right is reserved to refuse an application and change the terms of this offer. One application per household. Offer not available for current subscribers to Mills & Boon Romances. Offer only valid in UK and Eire. Overseas readers please write for details. Southern Africa write to IBS Private Bag X3010, Randburg 2125. You may be mailed with offers from other reputable companies as a result of this application. Please tick box if you would prefer not to receive such offers. ☐

mps MAILING PREFERENCE SERVICE